The

Freestyle

Cypher

The Suspense of It All

Kaylynn Hunt

Tanisha Stewart

Toni Larue'

E. Raye Turonek

Octavia Grant

Keira N. James

License To Kill

Kaylynn Hunt

The Task

Nick sat staring through his bay window. His mind had drifted off while his wife, Natalie griped about yet another thing he didn't care about. Sitting quietly, he focused on the neighbor across the street tooling around in his flower bed.

"Are you listening?"

"Yes, I hear you."

She droned on about the block club know-it-all, but Nick hadn't actually heard one word.

"Honey, I don't know why you let her upset you."

He threw the phrase out there just to double down on the façade that he actually cared. Nick couldn't wait to get out of there. He looked at his watch.

"Oh darling, I have to go," he said as he stood from the loveseat.

Natalie watched as he strolled over, kissed her cheek then scurried out the door. Once Nick made it to the car he waved as he backed out the driveway, the fake smile on his face beamed. A block away, if Natalie had seen him, you'd think he was a different person—, menacing. Nick drove just a few blocks away, he hit the button on the garage door then parked his sedan.

"It's about time you showed up," Terry, his partner, said.

"Look, you know I have to play my roll. I got here as fast as I could, you think I wanted to be there any longer?"

"Sorry dude. You drew the short straw."

"Whatever!"

At the time Nick signed up for covert duty, he hadn't bet on this type of assignment. And though at first, there was a bit of excitement, it had long since fizzled. The time had drawn out much longer than expected.

Nick sat there reminiscing. He'd 'bumped' into Natalie at a local coffee shop, they exchanged words and then laughter. When Nick and Natalie first met, he thought she was more beautiful than expected. Pictures hadn't done her justice. They'd actually seemed to hit it off. But after just a few months of 'dating' he realized why the pictures lacked depth. Because so did she. Aesthetically, she was captivating but inwardly, she was shallow, selfish, and self-centered.

Winning Natalie over had been the simplest part of the plan.

He wined, dined, and praised her right into what he wanted. Her trust, her devotion. A year into courting, he proposed. Knowing the way she held her father in high regard, there would be no way he'd let his daughter marry without being there to give her away. She'd told him her father was an important businessman overseas. Natalie hadn't offered any further detail into what that business was.

Nick knew.

It was his job to know.

After he'd wooed her into being his, three years had gone by. They were at the point of her trying to have a baby. Nick almost felt bad for her every month. She'd sink into sadness when her cycle came around like clockwork. He'd console her, reassure her. But all the while he knew the day would never come. Dr. Hanes had ensured that with the vasectomy he'd gotten five years ago.

"There she goes," Terry said, pointing at the monitor.

They watched the live surveillance as their subject entered the basement office.

"I'll be glad when this shit is over," Nick stated.

"Looks like your prayers are answered."

They listened to the call that was being made.

"Yes, Dad, I CAN'T wait to see you either," the subject said excitedly.

"YES!" Nick exclaimed.

Nick and Terry had been surveilling and waiting for years. They'd both taken the assignment with the mindset that this task wouldn't be a long road but enough to give them both the experience and notches under the proverbial belt they'd need at the agency. But they were far from on point. After all, four years had gone by and they still hadn't laid eyes on the target. But finally, there was a light. This tunnel was coming to an end.

"It's a go," Terry said.

He'd just reported to their superiors and gotten instructions to proceed with the objective. The widest smile crept across Nick's face.

"I have everything set to go. This calls for a drink." Nick opened the desk drawer and poured them both a healthy dose of Vodka.

Nick felt a wave of relief. It was coming to an end. No more hiding, sneaking around. No more lies. He could finally be with Mona. He closed his eyes thinking of how her skin felt against his. He was tired of pretending to be on business trips. Tired of lying to Mona about not wanting kids yet. She couldn't know he had a vasectomy. She'd be devastated even though he'd planned on getting it reversed. Mona was the best thing to ever happen to Nick. He couldn't hurt her like that.

After finishing out his night he returned home after his work shift early the next morning as he had customarily. Natalie was under the impression he'd just come from the oil refinery where he served as the midnight supervisor. She had no idea his nights were spent watching and listening to private moments. Her private moments.

The Target

Fredrico Julio Rumpkin was a man of international infamy. Was he the businessman his daughter, Natalie claimed? Yes, and much more. Not only did his company provide internet integration security to many corporations, he also provided many means for illicit transactions via its subsidiaries. He dealt in any and everything. From drugs, to guns, to money laundering, sex trafficking, anything.

Fredrico was also untouchable.

In addition to being a multi-millionaire on paper, he was a Chilean consulate member. Besides having diplomatic immunity, he was a very precautious person. He had not been in the United States in more than five years. His ties and back channels in the cyber community afforded him with access to not so readily available information. Information pertaining to an investigation into him and his businesses. Not to mention the numerous members of law enforcement that were under his influence.

But he missed his daughter. Natalie was his princess, his world, he'd do anything for her. Until his recent U.S. hiatus, he hadn't gone more than a week, maybe two without seeing her.

If they didn't meet for a weekly meal, he'd at least take her shopping, on trips. She could get anything she wanted.

The time had come, he needed to lay eyes on her. Several times he tried to get her to come to him. But her husband could never get away from work. She refused to leave without him. Fredrico tried to urge her to tell him it would be ok to take a week off. But he wouldn't hear of it, he had to provide. This husband of hers wouldn't allow Natalie to take financial assistance from him. Though she had her own nest egg, he wouldn't allow her to foot the bill. Fredrico admired that about him.

He decided it was time to see what this husband was about since he had yet to meet him. It had pained him to not be at her wedding. He'd planned to be there. However, he'd gotten wind that perhaps there would be an agent in attendance also. And though he knew they had nothing on him they could make stick, he didn't want to take any chances. The US government couldn't be trusted, their agencies couldn't be trusted. So, to that end, there was an emergency business situation which arose. It broke his daughter's heart.

Hopefully, this trip would mend it a little.

The Execution

"I'm so excited," Natalie stated as the doorbell rang, and she headed to open it.

"Dinner will be amazing, honey," Nick reassured.

Natalie greeted their dinner guest and then brought them into the living room where Nick was standing.

"Nick, I've waited so long for this. This is my dad; Dad, this is Nick, your son-in-law."

Nick extended his hand.

"Nice to finally meet you, Mr. Rumpkin."

Nick couldn't believe he was actually here. After all the times they thought they would get him. Here he was in the flesh. He looked much smaller in person, definitely slimmer but shorter too.

"Same here son,"

"Please have a seat. Let me get you a drink. Natalie told me how you like your scotch. I got a great one for you."

"I like you already, son. I'll take that neat. Rocks are for sissies."

"Coming right up."

Nick made his way to the bar, poured a drink, and returned to his father-in-law seated on the couch. He watched intently as Mr. Rumpkin savored his beverage.

"Daddy, tell me all about your trip," Natalie said full of glee.

Just as her dad began to speak, it seemed the words caught in his throat. He began to gasp.

"Daddy, what's wrong? Nick call 9-1-1."

Nick stood still. He was dazed.

"NICK"

He scurried to find his cell phone to oblige Natalie.

"9-1-1"

"My father-in-law has collapsed. Please send an ambulance."

Nick answered all the questions the operator had for him with a sound of desperation in his voice. Once he was able to hear the sirens on the block, he released the call with the dispatcher. As he headed back to where Natalie and her father were, he had a single thought.

That poison worked faster than I thought.

The Peeping Tom

TANISHA STEWART

Chapter 1

Marv peeked through the opening in his bedroom blinds, a beer on his desk table, music set to the right song and tempo, candles lit, and one hand already situated, fingers encasing his pulsing member.

Lacey was due any minute.

She wouldn't give him the time of day in real life, but with a little imagination, he could have her every night.

So, what, she was only twenty-five, and he was sixty-three?

"Age ain't nothing but a number, baby girl..." he breathed.

Marv sat there waiting, staring out his window through Lacey's open curtains like he always did, but as the moments ticked by, still no Lacey.

Lacey was always on time. Where could she be?

Marv grabbed his cell phone from the desk table and went to Lacey's social media page. She often posted her whereabouts, so maybe she left a clue about hanging with friends after work today.

After scrolling through her last few statuses, Marv saw that she had said she was tired and heading home after work. His heart leapt with joy because that meant in a few short moments, his night would be complete. Marv eagerly stared at his blinds, anticipating the moment she would walk through the door.

After another twenty minutes, Marv's high was wearing down. Lacey was pissing him off. "Damn millennials!" He grunted. "Entitled bastards, thinking the world revolves around them when other people have wants and needs and desires too."

Lacey was one of Marv's desires from the first day he saw her.

They lived in two separate apartment buildings sitting side by side. Marv's building was for people on more of a fixed income, while Lacey's was upscale.

"Bitch," Marv muttered, removing his hand from his pants in disdain.

He was just about to close his blinds and blow out the candles when he saw movement in Lacey's apartment.

She had finally entered her bedroom but appeared to be in distress.

The hairs on the back of Marv's neck stood up as he assessed the scene. Something wasn't right. "Why is Lacey backing in?" he muttered to himself as his panic rose. "Why are her hands up? Why is... oh shit!" Marv thundered, as he realized what was going on.

There was a man in Lacey's bedroom with a gun pointed directly at her head.

Marv's eyes bulged in their sockets as he became frozen in place.

"Lacey, who is this guy?"

His mind flashed to his cell phone. He could call the police and they'd be at Lacey's apartment in no time.

He reached out and thought to do just that.

Then he saw the man strike Lacey in the face with the gun and throw her on the bed.

Marv clapped a hand over his mouth. "No!"

He was mortified at the prospect of Lacey's perfect features being tainted, all over some young boy who didn't have any respect.

"Fuck this shit." Marv swept his jacket off the back of his chair with newfound strength and energy. Thoughts of calling the police erased from his mind. By the time they got here, Lacey could be dead. Marv might be eligible for retirement in a few short years, but with his military training, he still had some fight in him.

Marv cocked his Glock, ready for war.

He strode out the front door of his apartment to save his woman, whether she knew he existed or not.

Chapter 2

Lacey knew she had messed up now. She should have never listened to her friend Raesha who told her that taking niggas for their money was a good way to get over her ex. Lacey and Brandon had dated heavily for over a year until she found out about his wife and three kids. Heartbroken and devastated, Lacey found herself in a rut.

Until Raesha came along with a proposal. "Girl, Zaleik just gave me five hundred dollars!" Lacey had been vegging out on Raesha's couch after spending the night there after getting drunk. At some point during the night, Raesha must have slipped away because she returned in the morning all smiles and sunshine.

Lacey wrinkled her nose. "Five hundred dollars? For what?"

Raesha cheesed. "My light bill."

Lacey cocked her head to the side. "Bitch, ain't your electricity included with this apartment? And besides, whose electric bill is five hundred dollars?"

Raesha giggled. "To answer your first question, he doesn't know that. As for your second question, it's not my fault these niggas are stupid." Raesha shrugged like it was nothing.

Lacey wasn't done giving her the side eye. "Raesha, you worry me."

Raesha flipped a box braid over her shoulder. "Why? He's getting what he wants out of the situation, and so am I."

Lacey's eyes narrowed. "And what exactly does he want?"

Raesha sighed, her high deflating. "Damn, girl! Why are you so judgmental? Zaleik is a lame trying to flex for other niggas by having a beautiful woman on his arm. I'm helping him in that department while he helps me financially. Now he may not see things that way, but that's what he gets for trying to use me for clout."

Lacey's head was spinning. "Say that again?"

Raesha plopped onto the couch next to her bestie. "Listen girl, you may think Zaleik is one of the good guys like he was in high school, but now that he's grown and making money, he's feeling himself. He still has no game, but he wants to impress other niggas by having a woman on his arm. To him,

I'm nothing more than a trophy. So, my thought process is, 'If you want to use me for a trophy, fine, but you're damn sure gonna pay me for my services.'"

Now that Lacey was gathering her bearings, Raesha's story made some sense. "Okay, I gotcha I think… but what if you're wrong and he does genuinely like you? What if he gets upset when he realizes you used him for money?"

Raesha's eyes narrowed. "He won't be able to say shit about me using him for money because I already have proof his ass has been clout chasing. One of his so-called homies has been trying to get with me ever since he saw me with Zaleik. He spilled the beans about how Zaleik really feels about me behind my back. He called me a gold digger and all that. When I heard that, I was like, 'Okay nigga. I'm a gold digger? Show me whatcha workin' with then.'"

Lacey shook her head and laughed at her friend's antics. "Girl, you are one of a kind. I love you though."

Raesha draped her arm around Lacey's shoulders and hugged her close. "I love you too, girl, and that's why I'm trying to put you on. Have a little fun. Even though you may not be able to get your lick back from Brandon's married and trifling ass, you can get it back through another nigga."

Lacey was back to side-eyeing her best friend. "And how exactly am I gonna get Brandon back through another nigga?"

Raesha fake-sighed like she was explaining something for the thousandth time to a three-year-old. "Girl, must I spell it out every step of the way? Long story short, we find a nigga who's just like Brandon, then we get him before he gets you."

Lacey didn't know if it was the depression that had her agreeing to Raesha's shenanigans, or the fact that she felt somewhat justified in her endeavors, but she gave in. It didn't take long for her to meet Caleb.

At first, everything went smoothly. He wined and dined her, took her out on a date, and gave her money. Then when she used the excuse of finding out about his girlfriend and unborn child to break things off and block him, she thought it was over.

She got her money and her vindication and was ready to move on.

But Caleb wasn't ready to let her go.

And now here she was.

Chapter 3

Marv stalked over to the elevators, his body pumping with adrenaline. Gun in his right hand, he pressed the call button with his left pointer finger.

"Come on, come on…" he huffed, willing the slow-moving machine to hurry. Of course, it didn't. The elevators always moved at a glacial pace, which Marv usually didn't mind, but with Lacey's innocent and helpless features flashing through his memories, he couldn't take the wait.

"Fuck this shit!" he grunted, repeating his prior words. The stairwell was to his left and the EXIT sign blinked as if beckoning for him to enter.

Before he could form another thought, Marv was on the move.

Shuffling down the stairs at breakneck speed, perspiration began to pepper his forehead. His dress shoes swished as he halfway tumbled down the stairs. Marv silently reprimanded himself, wishing he would have changed into his running shoes, but it was too late to turn back now.

He hurried to the bottom floor, making it down within five minutes. Although his trek was downhill rather than up the stairs, the man still found himself winded.

Taking a few moments to catch his breath, he pushed the door open to get outside.

A gust of wind rippled through his silk dress shirt, once again making him feel like a fool for not changing into more appropriate attire. Marv was decked out in Stacey Adams, his favorite slacks, and his silk shirt that the receptionist at his job always complimented him on when he wore it. Marv didn't have a ton of resources, so he took care of his clothes. Now his favorite outfit was about to be ruined, but Lacey was worth it.

Marv snapped out of his thoughts and stepped out into the cool night air.

The sweat pouring down his back caused chills to sweep through his spine, but he shook it off. Lacey needed him - his comfort would have to wait.

Rushing toward the back of her building to climb up the fire escape, Marv gaped at the scene before him.

No one else was in the back of the building, but Marv made it just in time to see the man forcing Lacey into his trunk and slamming it shut. The man whipped his head around as if he heard Marv approaching, but Marv quickly hid, forgetting momentarily that he had a gun just like the young punk.

Seconds later, Marv heard the car door slam, then the engine cranked up before peeling off. Marv peeked out from behind the building with his cell phone in hand. pressing the camera button to take a picture of the license plate.

"Charlie nine two three Oscar four..." he rattled off, his military training kicking into gear.

Marv dipped off to his car, which was in the parking lot across from the back of Lacey's building. He tumbled inside and began a hot pursuit of the other vehicle, sending a prayer up to the heavens that the man hadn't gotten too far away with his woman.

After pulling out of the lot and going in the direction the man went, Marv found himself at the end of the street. At first, he was unsure which direction to go, but when he saw a car speeding up ahead and the skid marks on the right side of the road, he quickly followed.

His hunch was correct.

As he suspected, the black Mazda was about five hundred feet away. Marv couldn't make out the plate number, but his gut told him he had his guy.

A fleeting thought of calling the police and telling them about what was going down ran through his mind, but Marv quickly squelched it.

He was acting irrationally; a man of his age should know better, but Marv couldn't help it. He had to be the one to rescue Lacey.

Chapter 4

Lacey had never been more terrified in her life. The side of her head was pounding and bleeding where Caleb had hit her with his pistol, and her eyelids kept growing heavy like she would lose consciousness soon.

She suspected he'd given her a concussion, but she did not want to give in. She had to stay awake if there was any chance she would survive this night.

Who knew Caleb was a psycho?

He seemed like a nice man, or a lame, as Raesha would call him, but apparently, that was far from the truth. Lacey wished she could talk to her friend now and scream at her for getting her into this mess, but at the same time she knew she'd done it to herself. She was the one who sought him out, flirted, and gave him her number, knowing full well in the back of her mind that all she saw when she met him were dollar signs.

Were the two stacks he gave her for her alleged car repairs worth it?

Hell no, now that hindsight was 20/20

Fighting to maintain consciousness, Lacey's head was spinning. At that moment, Caleb went over a pothole. Lacey cried out, then bit her bottom lip as she tasted blood. Caleb was driving so erratically they would surely be pulled over by police, wouldn't they? If they did get pulled over, would he cooperate? Should she scream?

Hell yeah, her mind warned. She needed to scream if the cops approached them because no one was outside of her building when she was stuffed into the trunk, so no one knew she was kidnapped. Lacey couldn't call anyone either because Caleb crushed her cell phone in her bedroom.

It was her alone against a madman with a gun.

That thought caused Lacey to burst out in a fit of sobs. How had she come to this point? In the beginning, she was a woman looking for love, much like many other women her age. She watched as everyone else got married, had kids, and seemed to live happy lives while she looked like a damn fool when Brandon got exposed for cheating. She thought he was the one. He checked all the boxes. From the beginning of their relationship he told her he was different. His adamance about not being like other men should have given Lacey pause now that she looked back at it, but at the time she didn't see it for what it was. Brandon played her like a damn flute, and she was a silly schoolgirl, soaking up all his attention and affections like a sponge.

She had to give it to him though; he got her good.

Since he was a business executive, he was always taking trips out of town, so they only saw each other a few days a week. Lacey was skeptical at first, but when she looked up the company website, there were his beaming features. She even called his office for good measure, pretending to be a prospective client and then hanging up when the woman put her on hold to patch her through. Lacey had been burned before so she took precautions with Brandon. A bitter laugh escaped her lips as she thought about how all those precautions amounted to nothing because the nigga still turned out to be a liar and a cheater.

Needless to say, all those supposed business trips were really across town to his wife and children who were sitting pretty in a mini mansion while she lived in an apartment.

Once they broke up, Lacey moved to a new apartment for a fresh beginning.

"And now look where the fuck I am. Out of the frying pan and into the fire."

She allowed herself another moment of grief as Caleb careened around a corner, still driving aggressively. Lacey held out her arms to steady her body until the turn was completed, then she began to develop a plan.

Chapter 5

Marv had been into Lacey since they met but didn't think she would ever give him the time of day. As he followed the black Mazda at a safe distance, his mind drifted to their first and only encounter, outside of his nightly routine.

Marv didn't know it at the time, but Lacey had just moved into the building next door. He had stepped out and taken a walk to the nearby cafe to grab a coffee and donut and on his way back, they almost bumped into each other as Lacey was rounding the corner to enter her building.

"Oh!" Her eyes widened as she took him in. "I'm sorry sir, I almost made you drop your coffee."

Marv's entire world stopped. Standing before him was the most beautiful woman he had ever laid eyes on. He'd never been attracted to a younger woman before, and it was clear that this one was out of his league, but damn, if he could turn back the clock about twenty years…

Bronze colored skin, heart-shaped lips, eyes that slanted slightly upward, and braids that flowed down her back. Marv knew from the women in his family that the braids probably weren't her real hair, but he didn't care. This woman was flawless. Perfect. Who was she, and what was her story?

"Sir?" Lacey broke Marv from his mystified thoughts.

He snapped out of it. "Huh? Uh, yes ma'am, it's fine."

He couldn't help but grin. His late wife Mabel often said the thing she admired most about him was his pearly white teeth. Hopefully this young woman would feel the same way.

To his surprise, she smiled back and let out a giggle. That made his heart palpitate as a warm feeling swept through him. It was so strong it brought a tear to the corner of his eye. He had to know her. To speak to her. Even if she turned him down, Marv wanted to shoot his shot.

He opened his mouth to ask for her name and offer to take her out to dinner, but before he could form the words, she spoke first.

"Well, I hope you have a great day. Enjoy your coffee!"

Without another word, the woman whirled around and pulled the door open to enter her building, leaving Marv standing in the middle of the sidewalk, lost in a sea of emotion.

He thought about it all night and all day at work the next day. He had to see her again. If only the good Lord would allow it. There had to be something to the prick he felt in his heart. It couldn't just be lust or a schoolboy attraction. Marv was a grown ass man. He had been around the block plenty of times. This wasn't a regular hit it and quit it type feeling. This was real.

Feeling like an idiot but still hoping his plan worked, Marv purposefully took a walk to the same cafe after he got home from work. He sat at the cafe for a while because he wanted to make sure he walked by her building at the exact same time he did the day prior. When he exited the establishment, his head was on a swivel as he searched for signs of her beautiful features.

His heart lurched, then sank. There she was up ahead, but Marv was too late. She was already approaching the door to her building. Marv found himself speedwalking, hoping to catch her before she disappeared inside, but his heart sank further when she got to the door before he was within talking distance.

Marv stopped in his tracks as he realized he had lost his opportunity, but as if fate itself had woven their story, a woman that was in a passing car yelled out, "Okay Lacey! You're working that dress, girl!"

Lacey whipped her head around and waved at the woman as Marv resumed his trek toward her. She called out, "Thank you girl! Call me!" and waved. The car drove off, and Lacey scanned her surroundings, catching sight of Marv just as he locked eyes with her.

She was wearing that dress indeed. It was a royal purple color, fit for the queen she was, and it accentuated her skin tone perfectly. Silver bangles adorned her wrists, and she wore silver hoop earrings as well. Her lips were a deep purple color that matched the dress, and as Marv couldn't help but look down, he noticed the black high heeled sandals that adorned her feet with her pretty toes peeking out at him as if they wanted to be sucked.

Marv allowed his gaze to travel back up to Lacey's eyes, and to his utter surprise, she didn't look disgusted. Instead, she was blushing.

She gave him a small wave and walked inside her building.

Marv didn't get the chance to talk to her, but he had all he needed for the day. She blushed, and she waved.

She was his woman; it was only a matter of time.

Chapter 6

Lacey thought she had formed the perfect plan to escape Caleb, but as soon as the vehicle came to a screeching halt, all her ideas flew out the window.

Her body grew hot and cold as she heard his driver's side door open and slam shut, then his footsteps as he approached the trunk.

Lacey's breathing grew labored the longer he stood outside the car. Why was he hesitating? Did he change his mind about whatever he planned to do to her? Lacey prayed he did. She would give back the money with interest if that was what he wanted. She didn't know how he figured out that she played him, but he must have caught on to her game. That had to be it because why else would he hold her at gunpoint like this? They barely knew each other so it wasn't like they had a chance to build enough of a rapport for him to catch real feelings.

And judging by the fact that he began dating her immediately after they first spoke, he had probably cheated on his girlfriend with other women in the past. Why was he so hung up on her? It had to be that he figured it out.

"Damn, Raesha…" she muttered through clenched teeth, her fear rising by the second.

Without warning, the trunk popped open and once again, Lacey was staring down the barrel of Caleb's pistol.

"Why are you doing this…" She barely got her words out before Caleb grabbed a fistful of her hair and jerked her upward out of the vehicle.

Lacey yelped, the top of her head consumed with pain. If Caleb pulled any harder or caused her to lose her balance, he would pull her braids out.

"Please…" she whimpered as she struggled to keep pace with him. Caleb wordlessly stalked toward an abandoned building he had parked behind in a wooded area. All Lacey saw around her was darkness accentuated by trees. The nearest light gleamed in the distance but no one else was in sight to help her. A sinking feeling grew in the pit of her gut.

She was going to die tonight.

"Caleb, please…" she cried some more, but he opened the door to the building with his gun hand and sent her sprawling into the building with the hand he held her hair with.

Lacey scraped her knee as she fell to the floor, then she quickly flipped onto her bottom, scooting backward as Caleb slammed the door to the building behind him. The small room they were in was dimly lit by an upturned flashlight that looked like it was losing its battery. It kept flickering as it threatened to leave them in complete darkness.

Lacey looked from the flickering light to Caleb's sinister grin and swallowed.

When he noticed her fear, his grin widened. "Hey Lacey. Long time no see."

Lacey licked her lips in nervousness, unsure how to respond. She wanted to say anything she could to stay alive but wasn't sure what she could do to not set him off. Then it hit her: Caleb wasn't going to let her live through this. She knew his name and his face. If he let her go, she could easily identify him to the police. He was going to kill her. The only thing left to do was beg for her life. So, she did.

"Caleb, please…" she repeated her refrain from before. "Whatever it is you want, I'll do it. Please just don't kill me!"

Chapter 7

After seeing Lacey for the second time, Marv became obsessed. She had blushed at him — that had to be a good sign, right?

Marv went to that coffee shop for a third day in a row, but unfortunately, he didn't see Lacey at the appointed time. He was undeterred though. Creeping up to her building, he opened the door and scanned the buzzers for her name. Her building was fancy and had the first initials and last names and apartment numbers of the tenants posted. His building only had the apartment numbers next to each buzzer. After scanning the names for a few moments, fate struck again. There was only one first initial that was an L.

L. Rivers, Apartment 412. His heart skipped a beat. He had her. Marv stared at Lacey's name and apartment number until his eyes blurred, committing it to memory, then he quickly left her building and went to his own, traveling up the elevator to his apartment which was 414 in his building.

Marv counted the floors from the ground up in his living room window, then began scanning each apartment to see if he could somehow spot his woman.

When he did, he gasped.

Lacey's window gave him a perfect line of sight into her apartment.

As if sensing his gaze, Lacey looked out her window, but Marv quickly hid so she couldn't see him. After a few moments, he snuck and looked again and she was no longer facing the window, but she had a remote in her hand like she was deciding what to watch on television.

Marv contemplated his options. He knew her name, her apartment number, and now he realized he could see her whenever she was home as long as she didn't close her curtains, but after that he felt stuck. How should he approach her? If he did, would she give him the time of day?

"How can I find out her type?" he asked himself, then a lightbulb went off in his head. Social media! Marv mainly used his profile to catch up with family members and old buddies from back in the day, and he admittedly might have met a few women through the various dating groups on there too, but now his heart was set on Lacey.

Marv whipped out his phone and searched her name.

There were over fifty Lacey Rivers that popped up. At first, Marv was discouraged, but once he narrowed down the city and state, it was easy. He found Lacey's beaming profile picture in seconds.

There she was, fine as could be, and her profile wasn't private either.

Marv salivated as he scanned through her pictures. Most of them were tasteful, but she did have a few glam shots that she took for a friends' wedding and a couple of booty and cleavage pics. Marv quickly saved each of those to a folder in his phone. Part of him felt like a dirty old man, but he meant no harm. If Lacey ever gave him a chance, he would treat her right. He might have been almost four decades her senior since she was only in her twenties, but he had always been a good man. Never cheated and always took care of whatever woman he was with, including his wife. Unfortunately, death did they part when cancer took Mabel away from him.

A tear formed in his eye, but Marv pushed it away. Mabel would want him to be happy, even if it was with a younger woman. *Shoot your shot, baby,* he could hear her say. *Go on, I'm dead and gone. I told you before I passed that I wanted you to be happy.*

Marv went through a deep depression after losing Mabel, but he believed he would see her again one day. In the meantime...

He took a deep breath, then exited Lacey's photos to scroll her posts and learn more about her.

She didn't include much personal info — smart girl, but she did have her status as single, which was a good sign. And judging from the fact that she also was part of a few dating groups, she was looking for a good man. Marv joined one of the dating groups she was in and searched her name again. He quickly pulled up a number of posts and saw some of her comments.

His heart sank.

Just as he thought, Lacey was out of his league.

All the men she flirted with were her age and Marv was no match for any of them from the looks of it.

Sighing, he went back to her personal page and saw that Lacey had just shared a new status... *Ugh! If Only I had a man to buy me flowers...* Lacey had written the message as a caption to a post another woman shared about her man having done that for her.

The wheels in Marv's mind turned. "If it's flowers you want, baby, I got you."

Marv quickly went back to the dating group, remembering a post he'd seen as he was scanning Lacey's comments. The post asked all the women in the group to list their favorite colors.

Marv's eyes lit up when he saw what Lacey wrote. "Pink roses coming your way, baby!"

Marv pulled out his credit card and called up a local shop, scheduling the roses to be delivered the next day.

Then he refreshed his screen all day at work to see if Lacey wrote a new status.

Later that evening, he felt silly. Of course, she wouldn't update the status until she received the delivery - duh!

Marv had them scheduled for six pm, when he was sure she would be home from work.

Marv watched from his living room window and gasped in shock when the roses were delivered right on time. Lacey looked surprised and happy when the man gave them to her. When she closed the door she immediately put them in water.

Marv's heart swelled with joy. He had put a smile on his baby's face.

When Lacey grabbed her cell phone and began typing, Marv immediately grabbed his phone too, waiting for her message.

He beamed with pride as he read her new status.

Wow, y'all are not going to believe this! Somebody had pink roses delivered to my apartment today!

Marv grinned like a Cheshire cat as he saw that Lacey posted a picture of the roses with her caption.

The comments began flooding her post immediately.

Ooh girl, you got a secret admirer! someone said. A few people liked that comment, and Marv was over the moon, but his heart sank with the next comment.

Honey, you better be careful, someone else wrote. *How would they know where to send the flowers? It could be a stalker.*

Marv instantly became filled with shame.

He snapped out of it. Maybe his actions did put him in the category of a stalker. He hadn't meant to be, he was only trying to impress her…

His heart sank lower as he saw more comments pouring in with many of them agreeing with the woman who announced that Lacey might have a stalker.

Marv knew his chances with Lacey were up, so he resorted to having her the only way he could… through his living room window.

***

Marv saw the dirt road that the black Mazda turned down and kept going in case the man noticed him following. Once he drove for a minute, he turned down another street then re-entered the main street, prepared to go down the dirt road too. As soon as he hit the dirt road, he instinctively cut his lights, knowing what time it was.

This was a desolate area with nothing but woods and trees.

"Dear Lord, please…" Marv prayed. "Don't let me be too late."

Chapter 8

Caleb wasn't hearing Lacey's desperate pleas.

"Shut the fuck up!" he thundered, sick of this whiny bitch already. If she had known what was good for her, she wouldn't have done what she did.

It was bitches like her that broke a Black man down. Gold-digging thots with nothing to lose but everything to gain.

Because of women like Lacey, men had to watch their backs, always staying ten steps ahead so they wouldn't get destroyed.

Lacey thought she was smart, but she had no idea what type of man she was dealing with. She would soon find out.

He cocked the pistol, just to fuck with her, a taunting look in his eyes.

As soon as he did, Lacey screamed.

Caleb laughed. "Don't do all that screaming now! You weren't screaming when you did what you did!"

Lacey was so overcome with emotion, she was crying and snotting everywhere. "Caleb, please…" She could barely get her words out, her voice was so hoarse. "I'll pay the money back, I promise! I didn't even spend it all. I'll give you everything I have tonight and the rest when I get paid, I promise. Then we can forget this ever happened. Please, just let me live."

Caleb wasn't moved, but he did find her offer hilarious. He chuckled again. "Oh, you thought I was going to be the one to kill you?" He gestured at himself as he spoke.

Lacey looked confused, until she heard the slow footsteps coming from the other room. The woman looked so afraid, Caleb almost felt for her, but he was telling the truth: he wasn't the one who had it out for her tonight.

That job was up to his cousin Brandon, who just turned the corner into the room.

Lacey gasped as Brandon gave her a sinister smile that matched his cousin's. He was wearing black gloves and holding a rag in his hand. Caleb was confused at first, until his cousin gestured for him to hand over the gun. He complied, and Brandon wiped the gun down to erase Caleb's fingerprints, then handed him the rag. "Get rid of this," he said. "I got it from here."

Caleb cheesed. "Good look, cuz!"

Caleb quickly exited the building through the back door. He was halfway to his car before he felt a sharp pain on the back of his head, and everything went black.

***

Lacey stared up at Brandon in disbelief. Her eyes bulged. "You?"

Brandon continued wearing the same eerie smile Caleb wore. Now that she had seen the two men next to each other, she noticed the resemblance.

Brandon didn't answer; he just continued to point the gun in her face.

"Brandon," she stammered. "I don't understand. Why are you doing this? Who is Caleb to you?"

Brandon finally spoke. "Caleb is my cousin," he said. "I hired him to ruin you like you ruined me, but it turned out you were trying to play him, so we upped the ante."

Lacey's mind was swimming. "What do you mean, I ruined you? Brandon, you were the one who cheated!"

"Shut the fuck up, bitch!" he yelled, sounding much like his cousin had earlier. "As I said," he continued, "you ruined me. You found out about my wife and kids, and instead of just taking your L like any other jump-off, you went against the grain. You called my wife and told her, and she divorced me. That bitch got me for half my money and took my kids. And you thought I was just going to let that shit slide?" He said that last part like he couldn't believe his ears.

Lacey's heart thumped in her chest. "Brandon, you broke my heart! I had no idea you were married. I thought you loved me!"

Brandon let out a rough chuckle, mocking her words. "I thought you loved me! Get the fuck out of here. You knew what it was from the start. How would you ever think a nigga like me would want a ghetto bitch like you?"

Lacey forgot she had a gun pointed to her head for a second. "Ghetto bitch?" she repeated, with attitude, but when Brandon nudged her forehead with the gun, she fell silent.

"Yeah, ghetto bitch," he said. "You had nothing going for yourself. Working at a call center and going to community college. What the fuck could you have possibly brought to the table for me?"

Lacey's ears grew hot. "I was using that job to put myself through school!" she countered. "They have a program where they pay our tuition..." She stopped herself. Why was she pleading her case to this man when it was clear he had no respect for her, and much worse, he planned to kill her? She redirected the conversation, trying to talk him down. "Brandon, regardless of what happened, I never meant to harm you. I was hurt and maybe I shouldn't have called your wife, but that's no reason to kill me, especially when you were the one who lied and cheated. Please just understand that I acted out of hurt and nothing else!"

Brandon sneered. "You were hurt, huh? Well, this is about to feel a whole lot worse."

He raised the gun and Lacey screamed, but before he could shoot her, the front door to the building banged open and a man rushed in, aiming a gun directly between Brandon's eyes. "Drop your weapon, now!"

Chapter 9

As soon as Marv yelled at the young man holding his gun on Lacey, he heard the sirens approaching. He was relieved that he had called the police on his way there. He hadn't known there would be two men involved in Lacey's abduction, but his instincts never steered him wrong, so he followed them.

Both Lacey and the young man looked confused.

"Who the fuck are you?" the young man said while Lacey scrunched up her face like she recognized him.

"It doesn't matter who I am," Marv countered as the sirens grew louder. "The game is up, young man. Let Lacey go and I won't kill you."

Lacey looked shocked that he knew her name while the young man grinned, as Marv suspected he would. "You won't kill me?" he repeated, and Marv recognized the expression on his face as an act of bravado. The young man had no clue who he was messing with. With a cocky edge to his tone, the young man said, "Exactly how the fuck…"

A shot rang out from Marv's Glock before the young man could finish his sentence. Lacey screamed, but scrambled to her feet, running behind Marv as the sounds of the sirens indicated the police were right outside.

"I told you it was over, but you wanted to fuck around and find out," Marv gritted through his teeth, his expression stone-cold as the young man whimpered and panted, holding his shoulder but still clutching the pistol. "Drop the gun or take another bullet. Your choice."

The young man grimaced but held his ground. Marv shot his other shoulder, and he cried out, flipping backward onto the floor as the pistol went flying in the opposite direction. The officers barged inside, and Marv dropped his Glock, immediately holding his hands up.

"Lucky motherfucker..." he snarled under his breath. The next shot was going to be between his eyes, but the police saved him.

***

The next few moments were pure chaos as Lacey heard a swarm of yells, piercing screams of agony from Brandon, threats and accusations from Caleb, who was now in the back of one of the cruisers, and the cool, calm voice of the man who saved her.

Lacey knew the man from somewhere but couldn't place him.

While the police were in the middle of asking him a question, she couldn't help but to blurt, "Who are you?"

The man stopped mid-sentence and turned to face her, a shy smile crossing his face. He looked down at first as if he was nervous, and that was when Lacey noticed his shaking hands. He looked back up to meet her eyes.

"Lacey, I'm Marv, your neighbor... I live in the building next to yours."

It all came crashing back to memory. That was where Lacey knew him from! He was the OG looking man she had seen outside her building a couple of times. Lacey had joked with Raesha one night, saying he could get it if he wanted it. Her neighbor was the one who saved her? Why, and how?

Lacey opened her mouth to ask him that, but he spoke before she could.

"I saw the other young man take you and I couldn't let him hurt you. I hope I didn't overstep."

"Overstep?" she repeated, as if he had lost his mind. "Trust me, I don't mind at all."

Chapter 10

Marv was relieved that Lacey was okay with him saving her, but he knew the real answers would probably not be met with such welcome. He felt like a ticking time bomb as he answered the officers' questions truthfully.

Lacey was taken aside to answer a few questions too, then once they finished, the officers asked if they minded coming to the station to submit official statements.

Marv and Lacey agreed and found themselves in the back of yet another cruiser. Marv would come back to get his car later. Maybe Lacey would come with him and they would have a chance to talk without police around.

He looked forward to a private conversation with her, but now that reality was hitting, Marv knew there was no chance the woman would want to be with him. He wouldn't try to ask her out tonight, of course, seeing that she was so shaken up over everything that happened. Even when things cooled down, he couldn't see her giving him a chance.

What had he just gotten himself into?

Marv kicked himself for living out a fantasy. He was too old to call it a midlife crisis, but he probably needed to see a doctor about his obsessive tendencies. He'd always been a levelheaded man, but maybe his recent actions were symptoms of a larger problem.

A pang shot through his heart at the thought of being rejected, but at the same time, he had no choice but to accept his fate.

***

Lacey's mind was blown.

One second, she thought for sure she was about to lose her life, and the next, her neighbor of all people burst through the door to save her life.

The more she thought about it, the less it made sense.

She discreetly gave Marv the side eye. How had he coincidentally seen Caleb take her? Lacey had only seen the man twice and vaguely remembered him until he introduced himself, but he knew her name and everything. How?

Chills ran down the length of her spine.

Was Marv somehow in on this?

How did he know her name? They never had a real conversation, only hi and bye. The longer Lacey thought about it, the more concerned she became.

She hoped there wasn't something more devious at play in Marv's mind than what had already happened. When she thought back to how he burst in the room at just the right moment and then how he handled that gun so expertly…

It had been a long night.

Lacey wanted nothing more than to answer these last few questions from the police and go back home. But now she was afraid to do that because of how easily Caleb had gotten to her. The building was supposed to be secure, but someone must have let him in because she was walking toward her apartment door from the stairwell when he came up behind her with his gun. She didn't know how long he had been in the building or who let him in. Before she could scream or say anything, he was threatening her and urging her to go inside her apartment.

Fearing for her life, she complied, and then everything went downhill from there.

Lacey pulled herself away from her thoughts as they pulled up to the police station. She and Marv were taken to separate rooms to give their final statements.

When they finally finished, Lacey was exhausted.

Marv exited his room at the same time, looking equally tired.

"Did you need a ride home?" he asked. "The police are giving me a ride to my car."

Lacey froze. She wasn't sure whether she should trust this man, but her gut told her she needed answers. "Okay," she replied. "But can you drop me off at my best friend's house instead?"

Marv nodded, and they went back to the cruiser so they could retrieve Marv's vehicle.

Marv drove a Mercedes Benz. It was an older edition, but clearly well taken care of. The inside was clean as a whistle, and it smelled good too.

Marv held Lacey's door open, and she stepped inside and clicked her seatbelt.

The officers watched as Marv got in the driver's seat, then they followed them for a few minutes as they exited the dirt road and traveled down the main street toward Raesha's apartment.

Once the officers turned down a side street, Lacey faced Marv's profile.

"Okay neighbor," she began, her heart pounding in her ears as she was suddenly afraid and unsure whether she wanted to question him. "Now it's time for the truth."

Chapter 11

Marv tensed as soon as Lacey spoke. He knew this was coming, yet it still caught him off guard. He swallowed, then shot a glance at her bandaged forehead before turning his eyes back to the road.

"Are you sure you want to do this now?"

She let out a rough chuckle, which let him know he was in hot water. "No time like the present."

Never one to waste time or words, Marv pulled over to the side of the road. Lacey flinched when he unbuckled his seatbelt. Her hand gripped the door handle, but he held a hand up to stop her.

"I'm not trying to hurt you, it's just that I want to look at you while we're talking, and I can't do that while I'm driving."

Lacey stared at him for a few moments but relented. "Okay, talk."

Marv sighed. "Lacey, I am so sorry. Please don't see me as a creep or a dirty old man, but I've been watching you out of my living room window. Our apartments are across from each other, and you always leave your curtains open..." He stopped, immediately feeling ashamed and disgusted with himself. As he heard himself speak, he knew exactly how he sounded. He didn't even want to look in her direction anymore, so he looked down.

Lacey spoke in a level tone. "You say you've been watching me through your living room window, which is weird as fuck, but how come you never said anything to me? Obviously, you must have been interested. Why not approach me?"

Marv looked at her this time, exasperation in his tone. "Would you have given me a chance? Come on Lacey, you know you wouldn't. Once I sent those flowers and saw what those women said, I..."

Lacey gasped, and Marv knew he had fucked up even further now. "You sent the roses?" Her eyes widened, then another expression crossed her face as if she was putting two and two together. "So, you've been watching me on social media, too?"

Marv shook his head. "No, I only went on your profile one night, right after the second time we saw each other. I heard your friend say your name and I..." His voice trailed off because he was ashamed to admit the next part, but he knew he had to. "I went inside your building and looked at the buzzers. That's how I found your last name. I went to social media and found you, then I joined a dating group you were part of. That was how I found out you liked the color pink. Then when I saw your status about wishing you had a man to send you flowers... I'm so sorry Lacey, please forgive me."

He couldn't bear to speak anymore, so Marv fell silent. He'd never felt so small in his life. This was not turning out the way that he expected or hoped at all.

After a few moments of silence, he peeked at Lacey to gauge her reaction, but her expression was neutral.

"Well, the only thing I can say is I appreciate what you did tonight," she offered. "You didn't have to risk your life running after Caleb to save me, and you didn't have to..." Her lower lip quivered like she was about to cry, and Marv wanted to reach out and hold her, but his instincts told him that was a horrible idea.

Instead, he said, "Lacey, for what it's worth, I'd do it again. I know what you must think of me based on what I just told you, but I promise you I'm a good man who just made a series of really bad decisions. I hope one day you can forgive me."

With those words, he cranked his vehicle back up and set off for Lacey's friend's house.

Chapter 12

The first thing Raesha did when she opened the door, wiping her eyes and wearing a silk robe and headscarf was scream.

"Lacey! What the hell happened?" Her eyes filled with tears at the sight of her best friend's bandaged face and black eye. "Who did this to you?"

Now that she finally felt safe, Lacey stumbled into her best friend's arms, and they cried together for a few moments before she was able to pull herself together.

"A lot of shit just went down," she began, then Raesha closed and locked the door as Marv drove off.

They went to Raesha's living room couch and Raesha offered Lacey a blanket because it was chilly in her apartment.

Lacey gratefully accepted it, then opened her mouth to tell her best friend about the most bizarre set of circumstances she had ever encountered in her life.

"Damn, girl!" Raesha said when she finished. "This is a whole movie! And the Peeping Tom is the one who saved you? Wow."

Lacey was silent and Raesha seemed to sense something. "What's going on?"

Lacey was almost afraid to look at her best friend, but she had to let it out anyway. "Raesha, please don't scream at me. And I know what Marv did was creepy as fuck, but at the same time, when I think about how he stepped in and saved me tonight, and how he went through all that trouble to send me flowers that day…" Her voice trailed off and she didn't want to finish the rest, but her best friend knew her like the back of her hand.

"You like that old nigga, don't you?" she joked.

Lacey burst into tears and Raesha rushed to her side, half laughing and half consoling her. "Girl, simmer down. Ain't no shame in love."

"Love?" Lacey scrunched up her face.

Raesha smiled. "Well not love, but it was sweet for him to do that for you, despite the weird circumstances. I kind of see his point. Would you have given him a chance knowing he was sixty-three years old and you're only twenty-five?"

They stared at each other, both knowing the answer to that question.

"But wait…" Raesha said. "Before this conversation goes any further, let me see what we're working with." She pulled out her phone. "What's his name? Marv what?"

Lacey shrugged, not knowing where her friend was going with this. "Girl, I don't know his last name. Why?"

"Hmph," Raesha replied. "He ain't the only one who knows how to research." Within a few moments, she turned her phone to face Lacey. "Is that him?"

Lacey was shocked. "Yeah, what the hell? How did you find him?"

Raesha gave a nonchalant shrug like it was nothing, but Lacey knew her friend was secretly proud of her little detective skills. "I went to the first relationship group you were part of and searched his name. He was the only Marv listed."

Lacey relaxed. Raesha hadn't done anything advanced after all.

"Okay," her friend said, nodding in excited approval as she scrolled. "He's not bad looking, Lacey! Why don't you give him a chance?"

Lacey swallowed. Marv was easy on the eyes indeed. He had a salt and pepper beard and hair, but he was well groomed and kept himself in shape. Judging from his profile, he was also very family oriented and a former marine.

If Lacey were a couple decades older, she might have considered it.

"I don't know, girl..." she said. "That man is old enough to be my grandfather."

Raesha looked like she wanted to protest but decided against it. "It's your choice, bestie, but I'm just saying. Maybe this man is a blessing in disguise."

***

Marv spent the rest of that night and the whole next day kicking himself. He felt like a damn fool for what he had done, and then he confessed it?

What the hell had gotten into him?

"You didn't have to tell her everything," he scolded himself, but it was too late now. The truth was out, and Marv had to pick up the pieces of his lonely life.

The next day, however, he couldn't help but peek out his living room curtains to see into Lacey's apartment. His heart sank when he saw that she had closed her curtains.

"Good for her," he said, his eyes welling with tears for reasons he couldn't explain.

"Good for her," he repeated, and accepted her rejection in defeat.

Two weeks later, Marv was pulling himself together. He kept his mind focused on work and saving up for retirement. He was ready to write off his experience with Lacey as a misguided adventure, nothing more or less.

Then, when he got home, there was a pink square envelope taped to his door.

His heart leapt in his chest as he couldn't believe his eyes. "Lacey?" he whispered. It couldn't be her. She wouldn't write him. Not after what he had done.

Still, Marv found himself ripping open the envelope and feeling giddy inside.

A piece of a faded pink rose fell from the inside of the greeting card. Marv opened it and saw a brief message from Lacey, along with her phone number.

Dear Marv, she had written. *I figured any man who's brave enough to risk his life to save me is at least worth a conversation. Give me a call if you're up to it.*

Marv didn't need to be told twice.

He had barely let himself into his apartment before he was dialing her number.

After a few rings, Lacey's soft sweet voice filled his ears. "Hello?"

"Lacey?" His heart pounded uncontrollably. "It's me, Marv. I just got your letter."

"Good," she replied, a smile in her voice. "Well Marv, I decided I'm going to let you take the lead on this. Where should we start in getting to know one another?"

The End

Without A Trace

Toni Larue'

The Day in Question

Geri Ferguson pulled her mumu from her sweaty breasts as she planted her feet on the floor. A week had gone by without a working air conditioner, making sleep a mix of tossing, turning, and restless thoughts. The two fans she had on either side of the bed did little to cool her body temperature as they ticked, ticked, ticked on rotation, offering seconds of relief before her personal space was once again filled with unbearable heat.

The Bay Area had reached record-breaking temperatures over the last couple of weeks. The conspiracy theorist blamed it on climate change, while the church folk pointed fingers at the rapture. No matter the cause of the extreme heat, the fact was that hell had arrived on Earth.

With a stiff back and pain sharp like knives sticking deep into her right hip, a result of her sciatic nerve, she limped her slippered feet down the hallway to her son's bedroom. He should have been up twenty minutes ago getting ready for school, but his door was closed, and instead of the usual rap music that seeped through his confined space morning, noon, and night, only silence could be heard. A, *keep out*, sign warned her not to enter, but she paid rent around this mothafucka and only gave the courtesy of a loud knuckled knock before opening the door.

"Get your ass up, boy. You gonna be late for school," she said as she stood in his doorway. The lump on the bed moved like a blanketed glob as her demand was met with a slur of words strung together so close that Geri couldn't decipher one word from the next. The boy had been up allnight playing video games with his friends. She'd heard his muffled voice through the thin walls, cursing like he hadn't been raised right. "Get up," she yelled. "And don't make me tell you again."

Her son responded by kicking out his left leg from under the blanket. Even from the doorway, she could see beads of sweat on his upper lip like peach fuzz. She had to look into fixing the air conditioner, but the last estimate she received was four thousand dollars, which she didn't have. According to the news, the heatwave was set to last until the end of next week. *Maybe they could tough it out.*

"Boy!"

"Dang, Ma, I heard you." He threw the blanket from his body, sat up, and rubbed the sleep from his eyes.

"And make sure you get your sister up, too. Y'all think it's cute to be up all night until it's time to get up in the morning."

She slammed his door and headed to the kitchen to start a pot of coffee. In two hours, she would be in an itchy polyester uniform on her way to her job at the post office. The thought brought her attention to the pain in her leg. It had been months since she appealed her disability denial. The Social Security Administration had been dragging its feet on approving her claim. Her lawyer told her getting approved for disability while working was hard, but Geri couldn't afford not to work. So, she'd been forced to stand on her feet for twelve hours a day with nerve pain that no painkiller seemed to subdue.

"You didn't make breakfast?"

Darius' voice startled her from her thoughts. She looked at the clock on her phone. "You ain't got time for breakfast. Grab one of those Pop-Tarts in the cabinet."

He sighed as he reached for the cabinet doors and pulled them open. "Dang! Only strawberry?" He yanked the Pop-Tart box off the shelf and made a spectacle of opening one of the individual packages. If he only knew that she had to put back her yogurt so that he and his sister could have those strawberry Pop-Tarts. Speaking of his sister.

"Where's Chloë?"

He shrugged, focusing on placing the sugary breakfast in the toaster.

"What I tell you about that shrugging?"

"I don't know," he forced out. "I knocked on her door, but she didn't come out."

Geri stared daggers at the back of her son's head before pouring coffee into the oversized, you're the world's best mom, mug the children had gifted her the previous Mother's Day.

"When I make it back to this kitchen, you best be gone. The school bus ain't gonna wait too long for you, and I can't afford to be late for work."

She heard the groan of her eldest child as she made her way to Chloë's bedroom. Two years. Two more years, and the boy would be off to college. The hallway seemed to stretch for miles as dread filled the pit of her stomach. Last night before bed, she and Chloë argued, a heated exchange of words as the mother and child disagreed about appropriate attire for picture day. Geri had worked two doubles to buy the pretty pink dress, but Chloë refused to wear it. *You're an ungrateful little bitch.* Geri hadn't meant to speak those words out loud. She'd been wrong, but she had been so mad thinking about the pain in her hip as she helped one disrespectful customer after another to afford that dress. And she had taken that frustration out on her child.

The last words Chloë shouted at her were, *"I hate you."* Three words that would haunt Geri for the rest of her days.

Geri swallowed hard as she knocked on Chloë's bedroom door.

"Chloë, get up sweetie. They won't let you participate in picture day if you're late for school.

She pressed her ear to the door and was greeted by silence. Geri knocked again and then opened the door. The first thing she noticed was the beautiful pink dress, the cause of their argument the night before, crumpled on the floor. Chunks of hair that looked like spiders blew across the floor as the fan swept them way.

And was that blood? Smears of blood on the floor and the dress.

Geri looked around her daughter's room, fighting to contain her rising panic. The dread that had simmered in the pit of her stomach now threatened to spill over, consuming her with guilt and regret. What had she done? The world's best mom mug slipped from her fingers, crashing to the floor in a cacophony of shattered porcelain. Hot liquid splashed against her legs, but Geri felt nothing, her focus solely on the chaos before her. Blood, a discarded dress, chunks of hair - the scene painted a picture of devastation. Each repetition of Chloë 's words, "I hate you. I hate you. I hate you," felt like a dagger to Geri's heart, a painful reminder of how far their relationship had deteriorated. As fresh tears cascaded down her cheeks, Geri realized with a sinking certainty that those words might be the last her daughter ever spoke to her. Amidst the shards of the shattered mug and the remnants of Chloë 's presence, Geri felt her world crumbling around her. Chloë was gone, leaving a haunting secret that Geri would go to any lengths to bury, even if it meant sacrificing her peace of mind.

Thirteen Years Later

Geri Ferguson slowly stirred her tea as her watery eyes stared into the distance. Her son stood in the entryway, arms crossed over his chest, and by the look on his face, not too pleased that a detective stood in the middle of their living room.

"Sometimes, I can't believe it's been thirteen years that Chloë 's been gone," Geri said.

At the mention of her missing daughter, Detective River Mason stared at a shrine of pictures that cluttered the mantle above the fireplace. In one of the photographs, the teenager with bangs cut too short for her round face, frowned at the camera as she tugged at the hem of her dress. The detective's eyes bounced around to several more photographs and noticed Chloë hadn't been smiling in any of them. "Her birthday is in a few weeks." Those watery eyes held a faint smile as Geri took a long sigh before sipping her tea. "I buy a gift for her every year, hoping she will return to me one day. And I'll keep hoping until the day I take my last breath."

Feeling every ounce of his solid two-hundred and fifty pounds, Detective Mason shifted his weight from one foot to the other as he tried not to show impatience. After all, it wasn't Geri Ferguson's fault that he'd been demoted to the cold case unit and voluntold to solve a missing person's case that had gone cold thirteen years ago, all because of funding allocated toward the cold case unit. The local news was gearing up for a thirteen-year special dedicated to the missing thirteen-year-old. Like during the week Chloë had gone missing, the heat had scorched Northern California. Detective Mason wiped at his brow, noticing the warmth trapped inside the walls of Geri Ferguson's home, but only he seemed to notice the uncomfortable temperature.

"She hated those bangs," Geri said, noticing the detective scrutinizing the photograph. "I cut them for her seventh-grade school photo. She didn't speak to me for a week."

The Detective's gaze shifted back to Chloë 's picture. At the age of thirteen, Chloë disappeared from her home without a trace, only leaving behind blood smears, strands of hair torn from her scalp, and a crumpled pink dress abandoned on the floor that her mother said had been purchased for picture day. But Chloë never got the chance to take her eighth-grade pictures. The last photo of the missing child was the one with the bangs, the same one used during a statewide search. As he gazed at the image, a wave of conflicting emotions washed over the

Detective - the frustration of a case left unsolved, the guilt of not finding her sooner, and the fear of what might have happened to Chloë. Nothing else in Chloë's bedroom looked disturbed. The window above her bed showed no signs of forced entry. Maybe she ran away. Or perhaps something far more sinister had occurred behind the walls of the Ferguson house.

"Ms. Ferguson," the detective started, gripping a notepad in one hand and a pen in the other. "I know it's been a long time, but can you walk me through the day of Chloë 's disappearance?"

Geri's eyes met the detective's for the first time. She opened her mouth to release a chain of raspy sentences that sounded like she hadn't spoken in years. "I remember it like it was yesterday. I had woken my son up because he was late getting ready for school. I'd asked him to wake Chloë up so I could get a pot of coffee going."

The detective turned at the sound of her son clearing his throat and noted his jittery behavior. The young man had barely spoken to him as he stood in the entryway separating the living room from the dining room with his arms crossed over his chest.

"When my son came into the kitchen, I asked him where Chloë was, and he shrugged and said he knocked on her door, but she didn't answer." Geri took a small sip of her tea, first testing the temperature with the tip of her tongue. Those glassy eyes again stared off into the distance. For a moment, Detective Mason thought she'd finished her statement, but before he could encourage her to say more, she began to speak again. "You see, detective, Chloë was smart. She loved school. Was in the magnet program. Got straight A's. As a mother, I couldn't be more proud. I'm saying all that to say that Chole was never late for school. Rarely missed a day."

Detective Mason looked down at his notes. "In your original statement to police, you said you knew something was wrong. What made you think something had happened to Chloë?"

"Just a gut feeling. A mother knows when something isn't right with her child. And the fight we had the night before…"

Fight?

Detective Mason thought back at the notes the original detective left. There wasn't any mention of a fight. "What did you fight about?"

"Mom."

Geri's son's voice cut through the silence, but she ignored him as if he hadn't spoken. "I see her sometimes, Detective. She's never here for too long. But I see her."

"You see who?"

"My baby girl."

"And where do you see Chloë?"

"Here," she pointed at the floor, "in the house."

With a light sigh, Detective Mason tucked the pen and notepad in his back pocket. Clearly, Geri Ferguson was not in her right mind for an interview.

"Excuse me, Detective." Leaving his spot under the arched doorway, Darius approached Detective Mason, the scowl on his face showing displeasure. "Can I speak with you for a moment?" He gestured toward the kitchen, his movements tense with suppressed frustration. Once they were out of earshot from where Geri was sitting, he said, "Look, I know you are only doing your job, but is all this necessary?"

Confused, Mason raised an eyebrow, "Is all what necessary?"

"Dredging up the past?" Darius's voice was tinged with a mix of anger and despair.

"You're not interested in finding out what happened to your sister?"

"I've had thirteen years to come to terms that she's gone. And quite frankly, I want to move on with my life. We need to move on with our lives, and it's hard to do that with you and those damn reporters bringing up the past."

Mason glanced at Geri, who was now standing, dusting the cluster of photographs with an air of unease. "It seems she isn't ready to simply move on."

"She gets her hopes up every time you people come sniffing around here every couple of years, only to be let down. Since Chloë left, her mental health has been on the decline. I want her last years to be peaceful."

"Without knowing what happened to her daughter, I don't think peace will find her."

"She knows what happened to Chloë. She just doesn't want to accept it."

"Do you know what happened to Chloë?" Mason pressed.

"Chloë 's gone, detective, and she's not coming back." With a final glare at Mason, Darius brushed past the detective and returned to the living room. "I can't stop you from investigating, but you'll have to do it without our help."

They passed Geri on the way to the front door. She offered a fleeting wave, but her attention remained focused on the pictures in front of her. "Ms. Ferguson, if you think of anything, please call me," Mason said.

The brightest smile lit up Geri's face like a kid on Christmas morning. "I'll let you know when I see her again, and maybe you can help me get her back."

Darius's scowl deepened as he held the door open for the detective, the tension thick between them. Secrets hung heavy around them cloaking the room in a veil of mystery. Geri and Darius Ferguson knew more than what they were willing to share about Chloë 's disappearance. Mason stepped onto the porch, and with a sudden jolt, the door slammed shut, sealing in whatever secrets they shared behind those walls.

"You think you're slick, old lady. I heard what you told the detective." Her child's voice dripped with malice. His eyes burned with fierce intensity, a stark contrast to the child she once knew. Sweat dripped down Geri's face, not from the heat but from fear.

"I just want my baby back. Can't you understand that?" Geri's voice quivered, the words choked with desperation as she pleaded for her flesh and blood to see reason. But his retort cut through her like a knife, his cold indifference slicing deeper than she ever thought possible.

"He'll never believe you because you're batshit crazy," her son hissed. "And if you try that stunt again, I'll make sure you never see Chloë again."

The threat was as clear as day, a dark promise of consequences if she dared to defy him.

###

Detective River Mason couldn't shake the feeling that something was off with Geri and Darius's suspicious behavior like crucial puzzle pieces intentionally left off the board. The crime scene photos, witness statements, and heated altercation between Geri and Chloë felt like a tangled web of half-truths. Could Chloë have been a rebellious runaway, a product of typical teenage angst? Or had Geri and Darius done something to her? The haunting memory of Charles Bothuell, a boy who had gone missing for eleven days and was eventually found locked in a room in his father's basement, was a chilling reminder of the darkness that could lurk within familial walls. But thirteen years was a far contrast to eleven days. Multiple detectives had worked on this case, and the house had been searched several times. Surely, someone would have found Chloë if she were still in the house, dead or alive.

Detective Mason's focus was abruptly shattered by the jarring buzz of his cell phone in his pocket. Hastily retrieving it, he furrowed his brow at the unfamiliar phone number with the 510-area code flashing on the screen. Tentatively, he answered, "Detective Mason."

"Hi, detective. This is Hailey Archwell with KB5 News. As you may know, we are doing a sensational piece on missing teen, Chloë ..."

"I have no comment."

A pregnant pause followed before the journalist continued, her voice laced with amusement as if she knew a secret he wasn't privy to. "Actually, I wasn't seeking information from you. I may have stumbled upon a discovery that could interest you."

"So, you calling to give me information?" He asked. "That's unusual."

"I understand your reservations, detective, but to lighten your reserve, I'll admit I want something out of this exchange."

Detective Mason leaned back in his seat prepared to shut down Hailey Archwell's proposal. He didn't work with reporters because they couldn't be trusted. "Go one."

"Well, I've been assigned to put the piece on Chloë Ferguson together. Since her story has been told so often, I wanted to tell it from a different angle, so I began researching. And I've concluded that the Ferguson family is hiding something regarding Chloë 's disappearance. I was hoping we could work together to uncover the truth. I'll give you my information, but I want you to agree to do an exclusive interview with me once this case is solved."

"I don't work with reporters."

"You'll want to hear what I have to tell you. Trust me on that."

Hailey Archwell tugged at Mason's curiosity. Could she offer him the missing puzzle pieces he'd been looking for?

"I'm listening."

"First, I want your commitment."

He hesitated, knowing you could trust a deal with the devil before you could trust a deal with a reporter. But they were talking about a thirteen-year-old cold case with no breakthroughs; what could it hurt? "You have yourself a deal, Ms. Archwell."

He could hear the smile in her voice as she continued her spiel. "So, I felt it strange that out of all the interviews and specials done on the Chloë Ferguson case, the brother, Darius Ferguson, hadn't appeared in any, so I…"

"I spoke with Darius today. Let's say he wasn't very cooperative or pleased that I was *dredging* up the past. So, I don't find it hard to believe he intentionally avoided the spotlight. I hope this isn't the information you had to give me, Ms. Archwell, because if it is, kiss that exclusive interview goodbye."

Hailey was quiet momentarily, the silence more piercing than a scream in the night. "You spoke with him today?"

"Yes," the detective drawled. "Why do you sound so surprised? Part of my job description is to talk to people. Kinda like yours."

She ignored his sarcastic banter. "It's just that he made it seem like he hadn't spoken with anyone since being interviewed by the original detective assigned to the case. I wouldn't say he was cooperative. But he did say he can't wait for the truth to be exposed."

Mason straightened in his chair. "What did he mean by exposed?"

"That's the thing. He wouldn't elaborate, but he told me his mother knows the truth. She knows what happened to Chloë, but it's not what people think. He seemed relieved that I believed him and would look into it."

"Relieved? We can't possibly be talking about the same person. I was basically told to kick rocks before he slammed the door in my face."

"He slammed the door in your face?"

"Hmmm. He's a grade-A asshole if you ask me."

"Where did you say you talked to him again, Detective Mason?"

"He was at the house with his mother."

"That can't be right," she paused. "Darius joined the military shortly after Chloë disappeared, and he's been stationed in Germany. Detective, I don't know who you spoke with, but it wasn't Darius Ferguson. That's fucking impossible."

###

Geri Ferguson felt the crushing weight of her consequences bearing down on her, suffocating like a wet cloth over her face as she weighed the risks and rewards that would come with her exposing the truth. She'd held a secret for thirteen years to protect her child. The lies had eaten away at her mind like decay breaking down a corpse, and there would come a fast-approaching time when she wouldn't remember the truth.

She should have told the detective when he was right there in her living room, but fear had stopped her dead in the tracks.

Her heartbeat quickened as her old flip phone rang, slicing through the quiet tension. She looked at her door, waiting and listening for the sound of heavy footsteps. When she was sure no one was coming, her trembling hands lifted the phone to her ear. She answered with a voice barely above a whisper to guard against any prying ears nearby. "Hello."

She'd only spoken to him once, but his voice was as familiar as a lullaby. Detective Mason's voice crackled over the phone line. "I know the man in your home isn't your son, Darius."

Geri's breath caught in her throat, her heart racing with relief and apprehension. "I wanted to tell you, detective, but..."

"Are you safe, Ms. Ferguson?"

Her pulse pounding in her ears. "Not for long."

"I'm on my way," Detective Mason said into his phone as he raced through the streets, dodging vehicles as he sped towards Geri Ferguson's house. Before contacting Geri, Hailey had sent him a recent photograph of Darius Ferguson. Despite the man in Geri's home resembling Darius, there was no doubt that he was not Darius. Mason chided himself for jumping to conclusions, for not questioning further. He had assumed the man's identity when he introduced himself as Geri's son. After all, it was common knowledge that Geri had an older son.

Pure adrenaline led the detective back to the house without backup. Pulling up in front of the eerily darkened house, he felt an overwhelming regret. Hailey Archwell's urgent voice screeched in his ear through Bluetooth. "Don't try to be a superhero, Detective; call for backup."

"I can't wait for backup. Geri Ferguson is in immediate danger."

"How do you know she isn't playing you? She could be involved in whatever is happening. Just ask yourself why she stayed silent while you were there?"

He grappled with conflicting emotions, torn between his instincts that told him to trust Geri and the nagging doubts that lingered in the back of his mind.

Steeling himself, he cautiously approached the house, every crunch of leaves beneath his boots amplifying the tension coursing through his body. Based on the police reports, he knew the side of the house Geri's bedroom was on and hoped that she was there. He could see a low light coming from the window that should belong to Geri's bedroom.

He let off a flurry of light, knuckled taps on the window as a wave of unease washed over him, a sense of foreboding creeping into his bones.

"What's happening?" Hailey's voice was laced with concern.

"Nothing."

"I heard a noise."

"It was me. I was knocking on her window. Hoping to get her attention." Mason looked up at the window. The sheer curtains unmoving. "Shit," he cursed under his breath. Not wanting to alert the potential danger inside the house, calling Geri's phone was the last option. He didn't know whether she kept her phone on silent or kept the ringtone at a blaring volume. Mason raised to knock again. Only this time, he'd been met with a face in the window. He jumped back, thinking he'd seen a ghost, as Chloë 's face materialized in the window. But his eyes adjusted; he made out the lines in the woman's face with sorrow in her eyes.

Geri opened the window. "You're just in time," she said with a chilling cheerfulness that sent shivers down the detective's spine. "Chloë 's here. My baby's here."

"What the hell did she say?" Hailey's voice sounded panicked as she clamored for his attention. But even with all the warning bells going off, Detective River Mason found himself climbing through Geri Ferguson's window.

Once inside the house, Geri led the way down a long, dark hallway; each closed door was a potential threat. Not sure what could be waiting for him behind closed doors, his hand hovered above his service weapon."

Geri reached for the doorknob and twisted.

Mason braced himself, a breath caught in his throat, afraid of what he might see behind the door.

Geri pushed the door open. It moaned and groaned with every widening inch.

Mason caught a glimpse of movement through the crack in the door and used the tip of his boot to nudge the door open further.

He stood transfixed by the scene before him, his mouth forming a silent gasp as his hands fell limply to his sides. It was the second time he scolded himself for overlooking crucial clues that evening. But the signs were there.

Standing in front of the mirror, unwrapping an Ace Bandage from around his chest, was the man Detective Mason had presumed to be Darius. Jagged lines scarred his breasts…her breasts.

"There's my baby girl." Geri clasped her hands together with a smile so bright it lit up the room.

"Chloë?" Mason said, more so as a rhetorical question because no explanation was needed. The puzzle pieces fit together perfectly. And at that moment, Detective Mason understood - for the past thirteen years, Chloë had been living a life under a different guise, hidden from everyone, hiding in plain sight.

Thirteen years ago

"I hate you. I hate you. I hate you." Chloë screamed until her mother slammed the door to the bedroom. Life hadn't been fair for the teenager as she felt trapped in a body that didn't belong to her. No one understood. Life felt like a cruel cage for the teenager trapped in a body that betrayed her true identity. Bullied at school, shunned by her brother, and controlled by her mother's expectations, Chloë 's anger boiled over as she stared at the pink, frilly dress meant for picture day. *Fuck picture day.* She yanked at her hair, tearing out chunks. The pain mingled with a twisted sense of triumph, each strand declaring her rebellion. There was no way her mother would allow her to take pictures with patches of her hair missing.

In a moment of reckless determination, her gaze shifted to the reflective surface of the mirror, where she caught a glimpse of her budding form, hips and tits that she didn't want. Her hands trembled as she reached for scissors glinting menacingly in the light. The cold metal kissed her skin as she made the first incision. The blade's dullness, however, would only leave behind jagged scars. Crimson droplets fell to the floor, staining the delicate fabric of the dress in a macabre dance of rebellion. Each cut felt like a liberation, a step towards reclaiming her autonomy.

She collapsed to the floor and fell asleep, only waking at the sound of her mother's coffee mug crashing to the floor. You're the world's best mother. The lies shattered in front of her. The broken coffee mug mirrored the shattered facade of maternal love, setting her...setting him free from the suffocating expectations that had bound him for so long.

"And there you have it, folks. That is how Chloë Ferguson managed to disappear without a trace." Haily Archwell from KB5 News winked at the camera until they were off-air. She turned to her special guest, Detective River Mason. "Since the cameras are off can you tell me the name that Chloë Ferguson is going by now?"

"I have no idea."

"You're lying."

"I lived up to my end of the deal. You got your interview."

"But my audience wants to know where Chloë is now."

Detective Mason gave her a piercing stare. "Didn't you get the memo, Ms. Archwell?"

"What memo is that exactly?"

"Chloë 's dead."

Bestie

E. Raye Turonek

Chapter One

"It's gon' be alright, baby. Breathe… Just breathe for me." Chris professed as he pushed the wheelchair carrying his pregnant wife beyond the automated hospital entrance doors.

Lynn's short, panicked breaths gradually transitioned, becoming long, deep, and purposeful as she rubbed the healed over cut inside the palm of her hand. "Where is Robyn? She said she'd be here?"

"I called her. She's on her way, baby."

A mirthless grin fell upon Chris's face once he caught sight of Robyn whipping around the corner from the waiting rooms, the sound of her track pants rubbing together getting louder as she neared their location. She was just as tall as Chris, standing at 5' 11".

"I'm here, Lennie. Don't worry. You know I'd never leave you and my God baby hanging."

Lynn winced from the pain of the contractions but forced back wails and screams threatening to boil to the surface. "I knew you wouldn't let me down best friend.

They'd been friends since elementary school, the two of them. Chris not infringing on their picture-perfect friendship until college. Before his arrival, the women were two peas in a pod. Although it bothered him that they spent so much time together, Chris would much rather she be spending her time with her best friend and adopted sister than another man while he was out working hard.

Robyn slapped her hand on the nurse's desk, immediately garnering the attention of a woman in scrubs. "We need help here. My friend is in labor."

One of the women rushed around to assist. "Right this way, sir," she said guiding them to the labor and delivery unit.

After the arduous task of giving birth to a healthy baby boy, Lynnette lay in the hospital bed adorned by Chris on her right, and Robyn, on her left. She breathed a sigh of relief, comforted by having her husband as well as her closest confidante by her side. Even so, something was amiss. The look on her face as Chris took the baby from her arms seemed less than pleased.

"What's wrong, Lennie? He's beautiful. You finally did it!" Robyn exclaimed.

"I think I'm just tired," she offered up the excuse, while running her thumb along the healed over wound in the palm of her hand.

Robyn smiled. "Of course, you're tired. You just pushed out a human. Our lives are totally changed by baby Lance's arrival. That new beginning we've talked about since we were kids is finally here."

"Yeah… the new beginning started when MY seed arrived," Chris interjected.

Lynn and Robyn locked eyes, yet no words were spoken. Finally, Robyn broke the uncomfortable silence. "I'm about to step outside and hit this square."

The moment the hospital room door closed behind Robyn, Chris started in on Lynn. "There's no turning back now. Look what we've created. A perfect little baby boy. Our baby boy," he professed adamantly. Lynn didn't respond… "Don't tell me you're getting cold feet. We need this money if we're going to start over. We can't afford a house in California off my salary. Two's company but three's a crowd. I been telling you this for the past five years…"

"I know, baby. I just wanted to spend a little more time."

"More time?" Chris interrupted. "Y'all been up each other's asses since you were kids. I thought we talked about this."

"We did."

"So now you're backing out."

"I'm not backing out. I'm just…." Lynn shook her head in despair. "She's my sister and on top of that, my best friend, Chris."

"Adopted sister… And I'm your fiancé.

So, what's up?" Chris' eyes narrowed as if suspicious of Lynn's intentions.

"I love you, Chris. Robyn has been there for me through thick and thin. You have to promise me, it's going to be you and me for good. I can't take another one of your, she's just a friend excuses."

Chris shrugged off the completely valid criticism "I'm a grown man, now. That was back in college."

Lynn searched his eyes for assurance. "Promise me."

"I promise, baby. Let's just start over, me and you," Chris responded, locked into the intense stare down.

"Okay… Just me and you," she relented.

"No more Robyn…"

Lynn agreed, "No more Robyn."

That evening, Chris woke up by his fiancée's side, stretching his restless limbs. The fold-out cot they'd supplied him wasn't nearly as comfortable as the hospital bed where Lynn lay fast asleep. He took out his pack of Newport cigarettes peeking inside to find he had a couple left. Baby Lance lay swaddled in the bassinet at her bedside. He had time to take a couple drags, so he headed out to do just that.

Meanwhile, a woman dressed in scrubs rounded the corner, then into Lynn's room. Once the door closed behind her, she didn't waste any time. She removed the syringe from her pocket pulling the handle back to suck in as much air as it would take before injecting it into Lynn's IV. Not long after, medical staff rushed by Chris as he came up the hall to reach his wife's room. "We need a cardiac defibrillator stat!"

His eyes bulged from their sockets upon realizing which room they were headed to. "Oh my God, Lynn." He rushed to breach the doors, only to be forced back out by medical staff. "That's my fiancée! What's happening? What's going on?"

"I know, sir. But you have to let us do our job," one staff member rebutted before closing the doors in front of him.

Everything that could be done to try to save her life was done. Chris could hear them shocking her time after time in an attempt to stimulate her heart. It was too late. Lynn died that night in her hospital room. Her hand dropped to her side releasing a clinched fist. Chris could hear the long beep from the machine sounding off to signal her end.

"I'm so sorry, sir," a physician offered his apologies as he exited the room.

A downpour of tears flooded his face as he tore through the hospital, then out to his car in the parking lot. Once inside Chris let out an agonizing scream as he teed off on his steering wheel. After gathering his composure, he took out his cellphone to send a text to Robyn. 'WE NEED YOU AT THE HOSPITAL ASAP'

Meanwhile, Robyn wept as she ran her thumb across the healed scar inside the palm of her hand. She heard the buzz from her phone yet ignored it as she was preoccupied with thoughts of her late friend Lynn. She recalled the day they'd made the do or die pact to be together forever, slicing into the skin on her hand then shaking on it. To her dismay, Lynn had broken that pact the day she heard her vowing to end their lifelong bond outside that hospital room door. She'd trusted Lynn when they decided to get insurance policies on each other. Besties that would care for one another until the end, or so she thought. Do or die was the plan, yet due to Lynn's deceit, the latter won out...

Robyn shut her lids allowing tears to flow as she reminisced on fond childhood memories the pair shared. Their first encounter prompted by a whiff of fabric softener pervading Robyn's nostrils as Lynn walked by bookbag and cabbage patch doll in tow... The skinny, quiet, dark-skinned girl with two long French braids avoided making eye contact with other classmates as she made her way to an empty desk behind Robyn.

The teacher stood in front of her 3rd grade class scribbling her name on the chalkboard before turning to face her students. "Hello everyone. I'm so happy to see you all are here on time and ready to learn. You're going to learn and experience much this year. While I get your folders prepared, I'd like you all to get to know one another. Pick a person and get acquainted."

Robyn saw that as her opportunity to befriend Lynn. The smell of fabric softener reminded her of her late mother. Robyn was an orphan whose parents were brutally murdered in a drive by shooting. Although Robyn was in the car as well her life had been spared. The trauma caused her to withdraw from engaging with others. That day was different. There was something different about Lynn. She could see it in her hazel eyes. "My name is Robyn. I like your doll. What's her name?"

Lynn looked up, hesitant to speak, but forced out the words despite her reservations. She held her doll close, "This is Caroline Glennis, and my name is Lynnette. Most people just call me Lynn."

"What's that smell? You smell like the clothes my mama used to take out the dryer," Robyn replied.

Lynn smiled sheepishly as she unzipped the back of her doll revealing a stack of dryer sheets stuffed inside. "I wouldn't let my mama put her in the washing machine. My mama found a way to make her smell good anyway." She clung tighter to the doll.

"You have a good mama." Robyn attempted masking her mother wound, but a deep sigh following her admission divulged a sense of grief.

Lynn recognized that familiar sadness. She looked up and the words slipped out, "I had a good Mama."

The girls locked eyes. "Me too," Robyn admitted.

It was in that moment their bond formed. From then on, they'd mother and look out for one another. It was to be Robyn and Lynn against the world.

The memory waned as Robyn opened her tearful eyes, looked down into the palm of her hand and caressed her scar. Her phone buzzed. Chris had text again: WHERE THE HELL ARE YOU?

It was time to face him. Time to put on the greatest performance of her life...

When the elevator door opened Robyn was visibly upset. She rounded the corner to Lynn's hospital room in a hurry. The quiet, dimly lit room only occupied by Chris seemed colder. The bed was empty, sheets in disarray... "You're too late," Chris spoke up from the corner of the room. He leaned forward in the chair so that she could see him better. The distraught father continued, "They took her. You'll have to go to the basement."

Robyn scoffed, "The basement???"

"It's where they keep the..." Chris broke down upon reaching the end of his statement.

"Where they keep what?" Her face contorted.

Just then a nurse walked in. The documents she held looked official. "Mr. Lawson, I'm so sorry to bother you in your time of grief but I have some papers for you to read over and sign." She handed them over to him. "If you need anything, I'll be at the nurse's station."

Robyn squinted to read the wording on the first sheet. "Release of belongings?"

"Do we need to spell it out for you? She's dead! Lynn is gone and nobody can tell me a FUCKING THING!" In a composed rage he flung the documents to the floor.

Sobbing into her hands, Robyn struggled over to the empty hospital bed, fell upon it then solidifying the authenticity of her grief she wailed as if in pain. The way she'd begun to clutch her abdomen put the icing on the cake. Furthermore, her desperate pleas for her best friend to come back were Academy Award worthy. Her performance would do the trick. For now, at least...

Robyn's primary objective was making Chris pay for what he'd done. He'd ruined the life she planned by turning her closest confidante against her. For that he'd surely pay the price. In order for that to happen she had to be sure she'd gained his trust while becoming the solution for his every problem.

Codependence… financial and even in an emotional sense can be a powerful tool of manipulation.

Chapter Two

Robyn could hear Lance wailing the moment she entered the home. She tossed her car keys on the mahogany side table in the foyer as her eyes scanned its surroundings. There were empty baby bottles, bibs, blankets and even bound up pampers scattered throughout the living room to her right as well as the kitchen down the hall. But that wasn't where the screaming was coming from. Robyn rushed upstairs toward the screams to find out what was wrong. On her way upstairs she could hear the shower running. "This fool," she mumbled, rolling her eyes with exaggeration. Finally, she came upon what was now Chris's bedroom although he hadn't gotten rid of any of Lynn's belongings, as of yet. It had only been a few weeks since she'd passed. Even contemplating packing her belongings overwhelmed him to the point of tears. Neither he nor Robyn were ready to let go. She pushed open the door and her heart melted. Lance had broken out of his swaddling and his limbs were flailing about his bassinet as if he were a six-month-old baby. Robyn quickly scooped him into her arms soothing his agitation almost instantly. She kissed his neck and snuggled him close. "Everything's okay, baby. Mama's here," she whispered.

Robyn had the upper hand in the situation, and she planned to take advantage of it to its fullest extent. After all, it was Robyn who had the insurance policy on her late friend Lynn, not Chris. If Chris wanted a piece of the pie, he'd have to make nice with Robyn. A chunk of that two hundred-thousand-dollar policy could make a huge difference in he and Lance's lifestyle. Lynn's wishes were to be cremated and her ashes scattered in the ocean, making her funeral expenses minimal. Little did he know Robyn had plans of her own. Working from home gave her the time she needed to be the perfect crutch for Chris to lean on while putting her plan into action.

A few weeks had passed since the tragic death of his fiancée. Chris pressed forward in an attempt to be the best single parent he could be with the supposed selfless support of someone he'd always seen as a 'the third wheel.' Maybe it's karma, he thought as he stepped out of the shower comforted by silence and his assumption that Lance was sleeping peacefully. He wiped the medicine cabinet mirror free of moisture with a hand towel then stared at his reflection. "Damn." He felt pitiful. "This ain't how it's supposed to be. You were supposed to be here with me, baby. I just can't believe you're gone." Chris began to sob but, in an instance, composed himself. "Be a man, Chris… You gotta step up," he coached himself.

Upon hearing the creaking wood floor and the rubbing of windbreaker fabric he snatched his towel from the standing rack, tightened it around his waist then snatched open the door. "Who—" Before he could complete his query Robyn was pushing it open. Chris halted her advances instantly, only allowing the door to be slightly ajar. "You couldn't hear him crying?" She tried peeking into the bathroom. "Why don't you have the baby monitor in here?"

Christopher's face contorted. "Damn, girl… Back up. It is in here. The volume must be down."

"Well, you better turn it up. Anything could have happened. He was in there screaming his little lungs out."

Chris sighed, knowing he needed to do better. "Thank you for being here, Robyn. Lance needs you and I need you, too. I just don't want to feel like I'm monopolizing your time. I actually called my aunt to see if she could start babysitting Lance. You should have heard the way she got to squealing after I asked her." Chris let out a dry chuckle. "She'll be here today to pick up the extra key I left for her on the kitchen table."

Robyn felt like she'd been punched in the gut. Her heart raced and top lip had begun to twitch. She had to say something, and fast before Chris caught on to her shift in demeanor.

"You're not monopolizing my time. Lance is MY God son, and I work from home. It's not a problem taking care of him. Plus, he hasn't even had his six-week shots, yet. He shouldn't be exposed to all those germs." Little did Robyn know Chris was fully prepared to use Lance as a tool to guilt trip and manipulate her. He knew she wanted more than anything to be a part of Lance's life. He only hoped Lance's time was worth a nice payout. That life insurance policy would be paid out within the next couple of weeks. Chris could feel the palm of his right-hand tingling in anticipation of securing the bag.

"Well, just in case you need time to yourself my aunt will be happy to step in. She should be stopping by this afternoon. I need to pick up more things to baby proof the house and handle some other business."

"I can take care of Lance and visit with your aunt if you're not back yet."

"You're a lifesaver, Robyn. I'm going to get dressed."

Robyn headed downstairs to the living room. She placed Lance in his blue bassinet next to the sofa and began tidying up. She picked up all the soiled pampers disposing of them. Robyn swiped up every dirty blanket and onesie that could be found. She carried them to the laundry room just off the kitchen, her face splayed with worry as she tossed the clothes into the washer. She waited for an epiphany. An answer to her dilemma… Robyn opened the back door, stepping out onto the expanded wooden deck. She looked out into the dense brush, thinking about her late best friend. Tears flowed, painting her seemingly painless expression.

Robyn settled into her subconscious and 1997 faded into the background. A dark green Chevy Montecarlo bent the corner blasting "La Di Da Di" by Doug E Fresh & The Get Fresh Crew. Children waited in line at the ice cream truck just up the street. Some, rambunctious as they gathered while others waited patiently, arms folded as if in school. A group of about eight girls played double-Dutch not too far from where the ice cream truck was parked. The YMCA community center was a popular gathering spot for the neighborhood children. With children of all ages congregating, bullying wasn't an unusual occurrence. The heat was intense that day.

Robyn could see Lynn sitting alone on a bench near the little girl's playing double-Dutch. Most were between eleven and thirteen years of age. Two girls sat on the bench on either side of Lynn with intentions purely to annoy her for their own entertainment. Even at twelve years of age she was viewed as an easy target. Lynn was shy and standoffish unless Robyn was around. She seemed to be the only one who could loosen her up… the only one Lynn trusted.

One girl began twiddling with Lynn's French braids while the other picked at her doll's hair and attire.

The chubby fair skinned girl popped her bubble gum. "I wish my hair was that long. My mama said she just gon' get me a jerry curl," she confessed while teasing her short curls.

Lynn responded with *thanks* and nothing more.

"I know you don't think you all that." The light-skinned girl sneered.

"Dang! You do got some long hair," the skinny dark-skinned girl exclaimed.

Just then a child shouted amongst the crowd, "Open the fire hydrant. It's hot out here."

"I got something that can get it open," Reggie replied as Robyn came upon him. Once he laid eyes on her, he stiffened. "Hey. What's happenin', cutie?" Robyn smiled then whispered something in his ear. "What you gon' do for me?" Robin whispered in his ear once more. What she'd revealed had

Reggie grinning from ear to ear. "You got a deal," he exclaimed before rushing off.

Robyn pressed forward toward Lynn and the two misfits who were trying to get Lynn to get up and jump rope.

The fair skinned girl pressed harder when Lynn didn't get up. "Come on, get up and show us what you got."

"What's wrong you don't know how to jump rope?" the dark-skinned girl chimed in.

Lynn's stomach felt as if it were in knots. She could jump rope, but she didn't know how to double-Dutch. No Black girl ever wanted to admit she couldn't double-Dutch. That would be like not being able to braid or dance. In popular opinion those talents are part of a Black person's birthright.

The chubby girl's eyes narrowed. "She can do it. She's just acting fake," the girl shouted as she snatched the doll from Lynn's arms then tossed it out onto the ground. As Lynn got up to retrieve her doll the dark-skinned girl kicked her leg out in front of Lynn causing her to tumble to the ground. Lynn screamed as a piece of glass from a broken bottle sliced into the palm of her hand. Blood gushed instantly from the wound.

Robyn could see the melee carrying out as she approached. "Leave her alone!"

"Ain't nobody do nothing to her," the chubby girl professed.

"Yes, y'all did. I saw you," Robyn countered.

The girls stood up and Robyn continued her tongue lashing. "Y'all over here looking like the number ten."

A storm of laughter erupted among the crowd of children who'd gathered around. The chubby girl popped her gum then stood in front of her boney friend as if a Pitbull protecting its owner. With her right fist she punched the palm of her left hand. Oohs erupted among the crowd. Everyone in the neighborhood knew what that meant. A fight was about to go down. Robyn didn't waste any time shoving the bigger girl into the skinny one. She had a feeling she'd topple over crushing her protein deficient friend. The well thought out action worked. Before they could scramble to get to their feet Robyn yanked Lynn by the arm. "Let's go."

They took off but the other girls managed to scramble to their feet and give chase. As Robyn and Lynn passed Reggie standing near the curb she blew a kiss at him. His eyes lit up and he pushed the wrench with all his might, opening up the flood gates on the fire hydrant just in time to blow the number ten duo across the concrete and into the chain link fence behind them. Robyn and Lynn continued their escape as the crowd of children began to cool off in the refreshing but violent stream of water.

Lynn couldn't seem to stop crying, not just because of the wound on her hand but the one on her heart as well. She felt like an outsider, orphaned and unwanted.

"Lynn, don't cry. Everything is going to be okay. I promise."

Lynn wasn't as optimistic. "If it's not them, it'll always be somebody else," she whimpered.

"I won't let them," Robyn rebuffed. She took out her pocketknife, opened her hand then sliced into her skin. "Ouch…" she winced. "Now we are sisters for life." The two pressed their wounded palms together and the sadness Lynn felt melted away.

But that was then… Before her best-friend and adopted sister betrayed her. Simultaneously, Robyn swatted away a buzzing wasp along with the memories of the past.

Chris could see Robyn standing on the back patio through the kitchen window. She tossed a long stick off the patio and out onto the grass near the tree line. Chris knocked on the window then waved, beckoning her inside. "Do you need anything before I leave?" he asked as she entered.

"I'm good. You go do what you gotta do. I have some emails to send out and I'll clean up around here for you before your aunt gets here. I know she doesn't want to be sitting around no dirty house."

Chris sided-eyed the slick jab. "I'm sure Aunt Gloria would understand considering the circumstances."

Robyn raised her hands as if waving the white flag. "Oh okay…My bad. I can leave it like this."

It didn't take much time for Chris to reconsider. "I mean if Lance is sleep and you don't have anything else to do…"

"Yeah, that's what I thought." Robyn rolled her eyes. "You got enough pampers and formula."

"Booyah!" Chis opened the pantry to shelves full of formula, pampers, wipes and other essentials needed for an infant.

"Oh Snap! You actually organized it."

Chris tried his best to seem as capable as he possibly could. "See, that's why you need to chill and let me do my thang. I got this."

"Whatever." She waved her hand flippantly.

"Alright, I'm about to bounce. I'll be back by 7:30 p.m... I left the extra house key for Aunt Gloria on the ledge of the fireplace." Chris rushed to the bassinet to kiss Lance goodbye before heading out the door.

Robyn imagined Chris would be a good father and she could even see why Lynn found him irresistibly handsome. He had a nice set of tapered waves, a nicely trimmed beard and goatee, smooth mahogany skin and the body of an African God. Still, in the deepest depths of her soul she hated him for what he'd taken from her. She felt it only fair that he experienced the same betrayal.

The moment Chris walked out the door Robyn began her search. There had to be something there to prove he and Lynn's intent to get rid of her. She rummaged through dresser drawers in the bedroom, boxes of papers in the closet, even files and emails on his home PC. There was nothing... That was until she started to dig through Lynn's belongings from the hospital. Her cell phone had been powered off and stuffed into a plastic bag. Robyn powered on the phone and started with the messages between Lynn and Chris. It was within those private texts that she found the evidence she needed. The evidence proved the pair intended to get rid of Robyn and collect the insurance money. It was obvious that Chris had pressured Lynn for nearly a year before she gave in. Her reluctance to do so was apparent within their correspondence. Maybe she wouldn't have truly gone through with it, Robyn thought but quickly brushed it off. It was too little too late. Besides, Robyn couldn't bear the thought ruminating. The guilt would be too heavy a burden to bear. She had to proceed with her plan. Especially now that Chris had added his aunt to the equation. Since Robyn didn't have a way to record the messages, she took the phone for safe keeping. She was confident that the last thing Chris would want to do was explain himself to the authorities. Those messages would come in handy when the time was right.

Chapter Three

By the time Aunt Gloria arrived at 3:30pm Robyn's plan had been set into motion. She rushed inside from the backyard, scooped Lance up from his bassinet then held him snug to her chest as she answered the front door.

"Well, hello there. I assume you're Robyn." Aunt Gloria ogled Lance. "And this must be my great nephew," she cooed. When Aunt Gloria reached for Lance, Robyn backed up. The woman reeked of Estee Lauder perfume and Blue Magic hair grease.

"You should probably wash your hands first and cover your clothes with a baby blanket. He hasn't had his shots yet. His immune system is very fragile."

Aunt Gloria snapped, "I don't need you to tell me how to take care of a baby, young lady. I been taking care of babies since you were in diapers. I assure you." Aunt Gloria huffed, then brushed past Robyn to make her way to the nearest sink.

Robyn seemed to brush off the abrupt slight. "I made us some fresh lemonade. I figured we could sit on the back patio and chat. I was telling Chris that I have plenty of time available to watch Lance. He didn't have to bother you. Taking care of a newborn at your age would be quite the hassle, I imagine."

Aunt Gloria emerged from the bathroom with the saltiest of looks on her face. "It's no hassle for me, dear. I'm in great shape and I have plenty of free time to devote to my family. Christopher needs me so I'm here. Besides, I'm all the family he has left."

"I see." Robyn flashed a fleeting smile. "Well, I was just about to change Lance before his next bottle feeding. I have a tray of lemonade on the kitchen table. Would you mind taking it out to the patio? We can sit out there for a while so Lance can get some fresh air."

"Only if I'm allowed to feed him," Aunt Gloria reasoned.

"Of course... You can spend as much time with him as you'd like. I have a little more cleaning to do later. Between the two of us we can make this experience a lot less stressful for Chris."

"Then we're on one accord." Aunt Gloria proceeded to the kitchen to retrieve the tray of lemonade. Robyn cleared the way for her, holding open the screen door. Then she waited, silently. Not more than ten seconds had passed before she heard Aunt Gloria scream, then her body crash down onto the wooden deck. Her screams picked up and quickly became hysterical. By the time Robyn ran outside Chris' Aunt was being swarmed by wasps. All that poking Robyn did with the stick had already triggered the hoard into an impending frenzy. One they'd mercilessly unleashed on Aunt Gloria... Sweet lemonade dripping from her sundress only prolonged their attack. Robyn grabbed the water hose from the side of the house and proceeded to spray down Aunt Gloria and the hoard of wasps remaining. With the swarm nearly defeated and Aunt Gloria unconscious Robyn called the police. But, not before snatching up the thin clear wire she'd tied to the bottom of two wooden rails which had caused Aunt Gloria's treacherous fall. Robyn disposed of the evidence then notified Chris of the tragic events while waiting for authorities to arrive.

Aunt Gloria was the kind of aunt whose opinion mattered. Robyn couldn't risk her ruining the influence over Chris she'd gained. It was nothing personal, just necessary in her opinion.

That night Chris sat in a dark corner of Aunt Gloria's hospital room. She was the only family he had left, and he didn't even know if she'd survive the attack. He felt at fault for what had happened. Aunt Gloria was there as a favor to him. He swiftly wiped away a tear that fell from his bloodshot eyes. Now wasn't the time to fall apart. He sent a text to Robyn.

SHE'S STABLE FOR NOW BUT NOT OUT THE WOODS. I'LL BE HOME SOON.

Robyn replied without haste.

STAY AS LONG AS YOU NEED TO. I GOT LANCE. I'LL JUST SLEEP IN THE GUEST ROOM.

Her response was a load off Chris's shoulders. Maybe having Robyn around wouldn't be as irritating as he originally thought. "Ain't this a bitch," he mumbled finding it ironic that he needed the very person he'd attempted to get rid of.

Chris sat his phone on his leg, allowed his head to fall back against the chair and closed his lids.

By the time he woke up it was nearly 6am. Like clockwork the nurse arrived to check Aunt Gloria's vitals. "Good morning, I'm Margaret. I'll be the nurse on duty for the next twelve hours. If you need anything don't hesitate to buzz me or call me at the nurse's station."

"I'm actually about to head home and get cleaned up. I'll be back to visit my Aunt Gloria a little later," he replied.

The nurse smiled sweetly. "I'll take good care of her while you're gone."

"Thank you. She means a lot to me."

By the time Chris pulled into the driveway it was 7:30 a.m. Robyn's SUV wasn't there. He didn't find it to be anything to panic about. "Probably went to the store," he mumbled. Once inside he tossed his keys onto the side table in the foyer. It was pitch black. In addition to the curtains being closed, not one light was on in the house. He felt along the wall clicking on the living room light. "What the fuck?!" Chris's gawked with a crunchy expression, not understanding what he was seeing. Pieces of paper taped everywhere, along the walls, fireplace, end tables, even atop couch cushions. He snatched a piece of paper down from the wall. As he read, his eyes sprang wider, coming to the devastating conclusion that Robyn knew. She'd found out about their entire plan. Chris panicked. A barrage of thoughts raced through his head. Would she call the police? Where had she taken Lance? Could she be the cause of Lynn's mysterious death? Chris fell to his knees. His greed had caused a landslide of disasters, and he was living his karma. "No, no, no!" he shook his head, refusing to be defeated. "I can't go out like this." Chris stood, his eyes searching the room with intent. Thats when his eyes fell upon the envelope. Chris didn't waste any time opening it. Inside the letter Robyn explained her expectations of him which included him not coming after her or Lance. If he did, she would show the incriminating text messages to the authorities. Chris was expected to let Robyn and Lance live in peace. In a rage, the anguished father hollered at the top of his lungs. He had to find a way to stop her. But he had nothing to use against her. Just then his phone buzzed.

"Yes."

"Hello, Mr. Collins. I'm so sorry to bother you but we need you to come back down to the hospital."

"Is my Aunt Gloria, okay?"

"Sir, if you can get back down here as soon as possible we'd like to speak to you in person."

"Is she alive?!"

"Sir, please."

Chris slammed the phone down in frustration then belted out an agonizing scream. He knew Aunt Gloria was gone.

The walls had finally closed in on Chris. His misdeeds had come back to bite him in the worst way. He recalled an earlier memory from Lynn's pregnancy. She lay in bed beside him rubbing the precious bun in her oven. "Chris, promise you'll be the best father you can be for Lance. I want him to be strong, proud, and loving. An accomplished Black man..."

"I won't let you or Lance down. I'm going to be the best husband and father I can be," Chris responded before gently kissing her baby bump.

If Robyn thought she'd get away scot-free with possession of the most precious thing left in his life she was sadly mistaken. Losing Lynn had left Chris with nothing. However, losing Aunt Gloria, his only surviving relative, would bequeath to him everything she had left. That loss would be the financial gain he needed to track down Robyn and get his son back.

THE END but precursor to…

BONDAGE, a novel by E. RAYE TURONEK

Meet The Parents

Octavia Grant

"I am so excited that I can hardly keep still," Ashley said excitedly as she bounced in the passenger seat like a child.

"Ash, calm down. Your excitement is making me nervous," William laughed as he reached over and squeezed Ashley's hand.

The excited and overhyped way she was behaving was instantly calmed by William's touch. He always had this effect on her. He was a gentle giant. Calming and peaceful. His voice was so calming that it was damn near sensual.

For two years this man had been her best friend, her common sense, and everything in between. But as of yesterday, he was her fiancé. Just the thought of being the wife of such an amazing man, made Ashley beam with pride.

"I've never seen you this excited about anything. Well except the day we closed on the condo."

"I know I'm behaving like a kid at Christmas. I'm just so excited about the two of you finally meeting. I have never brought anyone to meet my mom. She thinks I'm a lesbian," Ashley laughed, though she was dead serious.

"When you see my mom, you won't believe that she's, my mother. She doesn't look much older than I do. But the kicker is her demeanor doesn't match her looks. She acts so old-fashioned. I can't wait until we get there. She's going to be surprised."

"You didn't call her and let her know we were on the way?"

"No, I didn't call her. I wanted to just pop up and surprise her."

"Ash, call your mom. Remember how we tried to visit my parents, and they didn't show up for about a week? The surprise was on us. You said she likes to go out to museums and brunch on Saturday. Let's check and make sure she's home. If she's not we can check into our hotel. I'd much rather detour to our room first and throw your legs over my shoulder," William joked.

"You are so nasty." Ashley blushed as she dialed her mother's telephone number. She was still amazed that this man could make her act so giddy.

"Hey Ma, what are you doing?" Ashley asked.

"Well, hello stranger. It's been a while since I heard from you. I'm not even going to mention all the missed calls that you never returned," Sharon joked.

"But I'm not up to much. Just cleaning these greens for Sunday dinner tomorrow. I'm going to meet Sable for brunch at noon and I'm also wondering why I don't have any grandkids yet. Ashley, I don't mean to start the conversation off by stressing you out. But I really wish you'd settle down, find a good man, and start a family.

After giving birth to you, I wanted more children. My doctor made it clear that he didn't recommend me having more kids, due to my diabetes. I wanted more babies so badly that I met with an agency to adopt a set of newborn twins. I bet my adoptive children would have already given me grandkids. You are always ripping and running, being a career woman. It's time you slow down and start a family," Sharon said.

Ashley shook her head and laughed. She was accustomed to this. That was her normal. Only her mother would have a monologue as a response to a simple, *"What are you doing?"* question.

"Ma, you have a grandchild. Didn't you and Danielle just have grandparent's brunch?" Ashley asked.

Sharon rolled her eyes and sucked her teeth. Danielle's father, Ashley's older brother Terry, was the product of an extramarital affair. Though she didn't want to, Sharon raised him because his birth mother made it known that she only got pregnant to trap Ashton, Sharon's husband. Sadly, it didn't work.

"God knows I love my Princess. But baby, you are my only child. The only flesh and blood that God blessed me with. You finding a good man and giving me a grandchild would truly be the highlight of my life,"

Ashley smiled.

She knew everything her mother said was genuine. She now felt even better about making this call.

"Well Ma, I have great news," Ashley screamed excitedly.

She couldn't believe that she was this excited. Ashley spent the first twelve years of her life watching her mother struggle, working from sunup to sundown. Living paycheck to paycheck, all while having a husband.

To avoid ever being a single wife and having to take care of a husband and children, Ashley threw herself into her studies, making sure to always study hard and remain at the top of her class in both education and looks. Ashley was beautiful, an exact replica of her mother. Her smooth caramel skin, full lips and slanted brown eyes gave her an exotic look. She paid exceptional attention to her appearance, being sure to maintain a healthy diet, a great skin regimen, and an active, fit lifestyle.

She wanted to make sure she always gave off top tier energy. She was only interested in attracting an upper echelon type of man. A man completely different from her father.

"Yes, Ma. When you speak, I listen. That's the purpose of this call. There is someone I'd like you to meet," Ashley announced.

"Oh my God! What are you saying Ashley? You better not be saying what I think you're saying," Sharon's elation could not be contained. She was so happy that she had to stand up.

"I'm saying exactly what you've been saying for years. Ma, truthfully, I was terrified to take any man serious. My first example of a man was not the best example. So instead of focusing on being a wife, I threw myself into my work and studies. Only dating casually, but-"

"Honey, I don't need the history lesson," Sharon interrupted. "Lord, thank you for delivering my baby from a future of loneliness. Tell me everything about this man. It is a man, right?"

Ashley threw her head back and laughed.

"Yes, Ma. It's a man. I don't know why you think I'm gay. We're on the way to your house now, if you're free."

"I'm free!!" Sharon screamed with the excitement of a lottery winner.

Knowing that her daughter was finally in love and in a stable relationship had her ready to jump for joy. All parents worried about their children finding love and happiness no matter their age.

Ashley laughed because she knew this would be her mother's reaction.

"We're pulling up now," Ashley chuckled before ending the call.

"Wowww!! I thought you said you grew up humbly. This house has to be at least 4,000 square feet," William exclaimed. He was shocked.

"4,972 square feet to be exact. This house is large, but I grew up humbly. Before my mom bought this house, we lived in a single wide mobile home in Landau. After my father died, she collected his insurance money and bought this house. As great as this home is, I was never impressed with it," Ashley admitted with a shrug of her shoulder.

"I know when you don't want to talk about something. So, I'll leave you alone. The home is beautiful though. Shall we?" William asked as he extended his hand to Ashley.

She gladly accepted. She was glad that William knew her moods and mannerisms. He would never push her to talk about anything that he knew could cause her mental anguish. She wasn't surprised that he hadn't mentioned her growing up in Landau. For one, he had always been wealthy. He wouldn't know what a struggle looked like even if he walked into the middle of it.

The main reason she was glad that he hadn't pressured her was because had he asked, she would have told him why she wasn't impressed with the home. She'd be forced to admit that something was fishy about the whole life insurance story. Before her father died, he was a bum ass nigga at best. There was no way he could afford a policy that would give her mother half a million dollars.

"I'll worry about my childhood thoughts later," Ashley said to herself as she raised her hand to ring the doorbell.

To her surprise, the door swung open before she had a chance to ring the doorbell.

"Well, it took you long enough to get here. Y'all come on in," Sharon said excitedly, as she ushered the couple inside of her home.

"Dang Ma! Were you just standing at the door waiting on us?" Ashley asked.

"You know me so well," Sharon joked. "Now enough about me. Who do we have here?"

"Ma? This is the man that stole my heart, the love of my life, my fiancé, Doctor William Hugo,"

Sharon's spine stiffened at the mention of the name, Hugo. Her heart rate sped up and her armpits began to sweat as she looked at the man in front of her. He was gorgeous. Normally, she would never use such a word to describe a man. But this man was the exception to the rule.

Tall, around 6'2"—athletic build. Dark as Godiva chocolate. Well maintained beard and his scent; Masculine and heavenly, with the hint of Sauvage or Creed. Whatever it was, smelled divine. It was distracting. Good looks and his good scent. His pleasant scent and good career were trying hard to distract her from the creepy sensation climbing up her spine. Because she couldn't help but feel like she knew this man.

In her heart of hearts, she knew that was impossible. This man was the same age as her daughter, but something about his fine ass was eerily familiar.

"How do I know him?" Sharon asked herself as she continued to stare at the handsome stranger. She had blocked so many things about her past out of her mind.

"Ma?!"

Sharon nearly jumped out of her skin at the sound of her daughter calling her name.

"My goodness, Ashley, use your inside voice. Why are you screeching like a banshee?" Sharon asked, gripping her chest to still her rapidly beating heart.

Ashley looked at her mother as if she were crazy. Ma, what are you talking about? I am using my inside voice. Are you OK?" she asked as she placed the back of her hand on her mother's forehead to check her temperature.

She knew something was bothering her mother when she switched from speaking directly to speaking in euphemisms. Though they now live the lavish life of luxury, whenever Sharon became flustered, she reverted back to her humble country roots.

It was as if going back in time mentally gave her some form of protection.

Sharon swatted Ashley's hand away playfully.

"Yes, I'm OK. No need to make a fuss over me. William, it's so nice to meet you. Please excuse my forwardness, but what do you do?" Sharon asked with a smile.

As gorgeous as the smile was, it was as fake as a $3 bill. She stared directly in his face trying to figure out if this was who she thought it was.

"William is the owner and head plastic surgeon of Hugo Body Cosmetics in Miami. Ashley said proudly as she grabbed William's hand and squeezed it lovingly.

"Hello, Mrs. Bright. I've heard so many good things about you. It's nice to finally meet you," William said as he extended his hand for Sharon to shake.

Sharon pushed his hand down.

"Put that hand away. We give hugs where I'm from." She smiled as she embraced him.

"Yes ma'am," William chuckled.

"I am exactly who you think I am. After all these years. Gotcha Bitch," William whispered so quietly that Sharon almost thought she imagined his words.

Sharon's blood ran cold. The sound of his low voice in her ear transported Sharon back to a time that she wanted to forget. For nearly twenty-five years, she had placed her past in a vault, hoping the secrets would stay sealed. But she could see now that vaults, for good reasons or bad, were meant to be opened. Sharon trembled. The feel of her quaking body made William chuckle.

Aloud he said, "Mrs. Bright, I've heard so much about you, it's as if I already knew you," William said as he pulled away from the embrace.

"I wish I could say the same. My daughter certainly kept you tucked away. By the size of that engagement ring, I can tell that we're ready to plan a wedding. I'd love to sit with your parents so we can get the wedding ball rolling." Sharon chuckled.

Ashley was oblivious to her mother's nervous chuckle. She was so wrapped up in the moment that she couldn't properly read the room. The only thing she knew was the two most important people in her life were finally meeting each other.

"Unfortunately, Ma, after all this time I still haven't met my future in-laws. They travel so often that we always miss them. With mine and William's schedules being so chaotic, we just don't have the time to wait around. I think they know their son is in good hands," Ashley said as she kissed the back of William's hand.

Sharon cringed.

Knowing who this man was instantly made her sick. She hadn't seen him since he was a child. Just thinking of the five-letter word: C-H-I-L-D made her nauseous. Sharon choked back the bile creeping up her throat as she thought back to the insanity that brought her and William together.

"Sharon, I'm working on an experiment. How would you like to make an extra tax free $10,000? There will be no paperwork. You do the experiment, and you get paid. Is that a task that you think you'd be interested in learning more about?" Dr. Norman Hugo asked as he ogled his housekeeper hungrily.

Sharon was beautiful. Her brown skin made her half Korean features somehow more noticeable. Though she was beautiful, her good looks had not stopped her hard knock life. As the daughter of an African American Army Serviceman and Korean prostitute, Sharon lived her first two years in an orphanage in Jinju, until her father found out who she was and brought her home to South Carolina.

Sharon's ears stood on high alert at the sound of $10,000. How her boss was looking at her, let her know some bullshit would be involved. But truthfully, she didn't care. Sharon believed her looks had gotten her into trouble more times than not. And she knew that this time would be no different.

"$10,000? What's the experiment? A threesome? An orgy? Sex with random men and your ugly ass wife?" Sharon said nonchalantly. She had grown accustomed to this. She was the daughter of a whore, so it was as if that life was destined to be hers as well.

Norman laughed like the evil genius he was.

"Sharon, you are beautiful. There is no denying that. But you know I wouldn't touch you with a ten-foot pole. Norman laughed.

Sharon rolled her eyes. But she did not rebut, because he was right. She had partaken in several deviant sexual acts in the Hugo home and though Norman had always been an observer, he was never a participant.

Norman was a disgusting human. She couldn't understand how someone as cruel and disturbing as he was landed a career as a Child Psychologist. Yes, Norman was a degenerate that masked his true heinous acts under a Doctorate Degree and brilliant smile. In Sharon's opinion he was a fraud. However, she couldn't deny that he had money. Money that she couldn't afford to leave on the table.

"For 10K I'll partake in this experiment," Sharon said shamelessly as she unbuttoned her uniform top.

Her days of shame had disappeared many years ago. Sleeping with different men, single or married, was her normalcy. Her daughter was the product of an affair. She felt no remorse for having her husband believe that he was the father of her daughter, Ashley, since he had her raising another woman's son.

"Good. As usual, I'll be observing. William come in here," Norman smirked.

Sharon's voice caught in her throat. Shock had rendered her speechless. William, Norman's sixteen-year-old son, entered the room, eyes to the floor, and shoulders slumped. He was an odd kid. It was hard to believe that he was even

Norman's son. He had absolutely no swagger about him. Sharon quickly grabbed her shirt to hide her large breast.

"Sir, are you insane? William is a child. I have a daughter a few years younger than him. I'm twice his age!" Sharon screamed.

Norman was not impressed with her show of disdain.

"My son is sixteen. In thirty-one states, the age of consent is sixteen,"

"I am aware that thirty-one states have that age of consent. But the age of consent in this state is eighteen!" she countered.

"Sharon, it is time for my son to know the feel of a woman. He will be seventeen in two weeks and has never experienced coitus. I have no problem throwing in an extra $2,000-$3,000 if that sweetens the pot for you," Norman said as he went into the pocket of his lab jacket and flung stacks of money at her feet.

Sharon wanted to resist, she wanted to say no, but the green faces staring back at her moved her feet. That day, thirty-two-year-old Sharon did things to William that he was not ready for.

Norman wrote the following in his experiment notes: Women that live paycheck to paycheck lack morals. They are willing to break the law if the money is right.

The memories of her past made Sharon sick. She prayed that Ashley never found out about the type of woman she used to be. The fact that William was now with her daughter, and could potentially spill the beans, made Sharon...

BLAH!!!

Hot bile ran a race up Sharon's throat and forced itself between her lips and through her nose. She didn't have time to make it to the trash or the sink. All of the contents of her stomach were now on the front of her clothes and the floor.

"Mom! Oh my God! Are you ok?" Ashley asked as she rushed to her mother's side. Worry instantly creased Ashley's wrinkle free face. Her mother was just in a great mood. So, she couldn't understand what had happened in the five minutes they'd been talking.

Sharon gagged and dry heaved before she could form enough words to speak.

"I'm so sorry. I think the dairy that I used in the Mac & Cheese is spoiled. That milk did taste a little funny to me," Sharon lied.

"Dairy in the Mac & cheese?" Ashley repeated with a scrunched face, "Ma, you look like you just aged ten years in five minutes," she said as she grabbed the apron from the bar and threw it on top of the vomit.

Sharon was well over fifty years old, but she didn't look a day over thirty. Her beauty was truly ageless.

"Girl, stop fussing over me. I'm ok," Sharon lied.

The grotesque knowing smile on William's face instantly made her sick again.

Remembering how William used to trail her around the house like a stalker staring at her without blinking made her skin crawl. Though she wasn't proud of the act, she needed the money. She simply told herself, this is legal in some states, and moved on.

The day Norman and his family left for vacation to Turks, Sharon raided the safe of $500,000 and moved her and her daughter out of South Carolina. The mere sight of William made Sharon vomit once again.

"Ma, Oh my goodness! Will, I have my medical bag in the car. Can you run out and get it and check her vitals? I'm going to run downstairs to the laundry room and get some towels and cleaning supplies.

Sharon instantly hated having the laundry room and cleaning supplies downstairs. After buying her own home she hired someone else to clean for her. She didn't want to be next to any cleaning supplies. Now because of her, "This is beneath me" mentality, she was in the same space as the person that made her life hell.

"William, I-"

Before Sharon could finish whatever lie she planned to tell, William grabbed her by her throat and slammed her onto the marble countertop. With his right hand he quickly unzipped his pants and rammed his hard dick inside of his soon to be mother-in-law. He didn't care that his soon-to-be-wife was downstairs. He didn't care that she was covered in vomit. All he cared about was being balls deep inside the woman that he loved since he was sixteen.

"Remember all the nasty shit you used to do to me, huh? Now you want to act like you don't remember me." William said, as he slammed into Sharon with the speed of a jackrabbit.

"In the middle of doing things you knew I couldn't resist; you said if I got rid of your worthless husband, you and I could be together forever," William moaned as he continued to pump wildly while rubbing Sharon's clitoris like she taught him.

"I laced Ashton's drink like you told me and ran him over like we discussed, and instead of us running off together, you ran off with my college tuition! You pretty, sneaky, lying bitch!" William screamed silently as he continued to pump aggressively. The same way he did when he lost his virginity.

Sharon cried. She could not believe her past had caught up to her like this.

"God please help me. Please fix this! Don't let my daughter get hurt by this maniac." Sharon prayed as the person she assaulted twenty-five years ago, assaulted her.

"They say you never forget your first. You took my virginity, my love, and my college tuition. I'm going to enjoy fucking my $500,000 out of your pretty, trifling ass. I bet Ashley doesn't even know how fucked up you are. All I kept hearing is, I can't wait until you meet my mom," William taunted as he released a walnut sized load into Sharon's unresponsive vag.

He ignored her face full of tears. Her feelings were not important. Instead, he focused on the hardness that remained in his dick. Sharon was a snake, but she was too damn pretty.

"I'ma fuck you in your ass. You used to like that you freak bitch. I'll make Ashley's prude ass suck it later. I guess I have to tell her how her mama gets down, so she'll loosen up in the bedroom," William laughed maniacally as he positioned his bare erection at Sharon's back door.

"If you scream, I'll have to kill that uppity bitch! Just like I did her daddy," William said as he placed his hand over Sharon's mouth as he attempted to push all eight inches inside of her anal canal.

Sharon was in hell. She cried openly as this man that was supposed to be her son in law took advantage of her.

The sound of Ashley's footsteps and the clanging of the mop bucket hitting the wall as she ascended the stairs was the only thing that made William stop his brutal assault.

"Saved by the bell, bitch!" William said through clenched teeth as he fought to tuck his man of steel into his slacks.

Sharon whimpered. She fought hard to hold her emotions in. She had been a part of some truly scandalous deeds in her life: robbery, identity theft, and accessory to murder. Though those acts were heinous, she never expected to be raped. She felt empty. Shame, unlike anything she had ever felt seized her. The trauma of it all left her speechless. There was no way she could face her daughter after this. With the speed of a cheetah, Sharon ran to her bedroom.

William wanted to burst into laughter at the sight of Sharon scurrying off. The only thing that kept the laughter from bursting out of his mouth was the fact that he could hear Ashley approaching.

"I'm sorry it took so long. The light bulb is out in the laundry room. I had to use my cell phone flashlight, and it was still dark. Where'd my mom go?" Ashley asked once she made it back into the kitchen. She smiled when she saw her man wearing yellow gloves and spraying the counter down with disinfectant.

"Babe, you didn't have to clean up in here," Ashley said. She could not get over how amazing this man was.

"It's fine, Ash. It's just vomit. I see it every day. After BBL's, lipo, and tummy tucks, women become nauseous. But this case is different. Your mom really did make the macaroni with spoiled milk," William stated as he held up the carton of milk.

"A few other items in the fridge are outdated also. If you want, we can stay here tonight, that way you can keep an eye on her. Then we can go grocery shopping for her tomorrow," William said sounding like the loving fiancé that he was not.

"Are you serious, Will? You don't mind if we miss our reservations?"

"No, she's your mom. I know you're going to be worried about her. I'd be as worried as you are if it were my mom. I'll go get our bags out of the trunk and we can camp out here."

"You're the best. Let me clean this mess up, then I'll show you my old room," Ashley said as she prepared to clean the kitchen.

William smirked. Logging into the sideline app, William altered his cellphone number to call Sharon. He knew that if she saw 305, she wouldn't answer the phone. So, he opted to select a number with an 864area code.

"Hello?"

The tears in Sharon's voice meant nothing to him.

"Unless you want your daughter to find out the type of mother you really are, I suggest you leave that bedroom door unlocked. We're spending the night. I plan to come in your room and get some more of that pussy later.

*****

Six months later...

William sat at the table digging into his dessert first. He was as happy as a clam as he ate his decadent strawberry pudding cake. Things had really been going well with him. He had been laying dick to Sharon at least three times a month. Using his frequent flier miles to get to her in record time. His relationship with Ashley was perfect, and he was on a new medication that stopped his mood swings. All in all, life for William was great.

"I see you're in a good mood," Ashley said as she watched her fiancé do a happy dance as he ate his dessert before the entrée.

"I am. Things have been going great at work. More clients have been coming in due to the summer sales ads, I brought on three more qualified doctors, and most importantly, we finally set a date." William smiled as he took a bite of his sugary treat.

He refused to say things were great because he was also having sex with her mother. No, that was his personal business and did not concern his future wife.

Ashley was glad to see him like this. She knew now would be the best time to say what she needed to say.

"Babe, since we have set a date, and that date is approaching, I think it's time that I met your parents," Ashley said meekly.

To anyone sitting in the exquisitely decorated candlelit restaurant, the young couple sitting at the table were simply having a normal conversation over a romantic dinner. But that was not the case.

Her casual statement nearly made William choke on his Cabernet Sauvignon. Ashley knew what she was asking was major. She hoped that the serene atmosphere and public setting would keep William calm. He was always calm and laid back but talk of his parents always ruffled his feathers.

For the past couple of years, there was always an excuse as to why she couldn't meet them: they were on vacation, at a medical convention, or simply not accepting visitors. Anytime they went by his parents' home, she was asked to stay in the car. Ashley didn't understand why it seemed next to impossible to meet the family that she was about to be married into.

"Where did that come from?" William asked after clearing his throat of the wine that nearly choked him to death.

"What do you mean where did it come from? William, we've been dating for two and a half years. We've taken exquisite trips around the world, we're about to get married, and we're trying to have a baby. We've accomplished so many great things, but I know absolutely nothing about your parents.

The last picture I've seen of them was from ten years ago. They're not on social media or anything. It's strange that I have to beg to meet my in-laws. You've met my mom. So why is it that when I ask to meet your family there's a reason why I can't. Are you ashamed of me?" Ashley asked somberly.

William's heart sank. As crazy as his antics were, he had to admit that he did love Ashley. Just not enough to stop forcing sex on her mother or allow her to meet his parents.

"Ashley Renee Bright, you are amazing. Everything about you is perfect. It's not that I don't think you're good enough. Truthfully Ash, they aren't good enough to meet you. My parents aren't worthy enough to grace your presence," William said as he grabbed her hand and kissed it.

As he spoke, his outside persona remained caring. But on the inside his anger grew like a raging fire. He fought hard to keep his ill feelings in check but knew it was a battle that he probably wouldn't win.

"How dare this bitch question me?" He thought as he lovingly kissed the palm of her hand.

"Will, you've admitted that the relationship between yourself and your parents wasn't the best. I get that. Before my dad died, our relationship was sour. But I had to forgive him so I could find peace in my life. And without my mom, I'd die. There's nothing she could do that would ever make me hate her.

At some point, you have to let that hurt go. I think we should look into therapy."

William bristled.

"Ashley, it's not that easy to just move on from some things. Now, can we just drop the subject and enjoy our meal?" he said as he wiped his forehead of the perspiration that suddenly appeared.

"You don't know the half of how fucked up your mother is. If you knew the truth, you'd shut the fuck up," William thought as he fought to control the fire that was burning inside of him. He fought to control his breathing and the shakes that were threatening to consume his body. This was a clear sign that he had forgotten to take his Lithium.

Ashley sighed.

"This is just crazy to me. We bought a home together, I'm a joint user on your checking and savings account. I don't understand how you could trust me with your money and your home but not want me to meet your family. Look, the other night I heard you saying you needed to be at your parents' house to sign for your delivery. Since, I want to meet my future in laws, I went to their house but-"

"You did what?" William screamed as he hopped out of his chair.

He stood up with so much force that the chair fell over, and the table shook. Ashley's eyes grew to the size of golf balls. She had never seen him like this. She instantly knew that she had fucked up.

"William, I... I'm sorry. I just..."

"You just what? You just thought it was a good idea to go behind my back and do something that you knew I wouldn't like?" he screamed.

Like a rabid dog, white foam showed at the corners of his mouth. The patrons of the restaurant stopped chattering and stared at the young couple.

"Baby, I'm sorry. It'll never happen again. Forget I said anything," Ashley stuttered.

She was so scared that she wanted to run away. She thought that if she told him what she had done in public that he'd be calm, but she could see now that she was dead wrong.

"William. I'm sorry. Just forget..."

"Forget what? You know what, since you want to meet my parents so badly. Let's go," William said, as he grabbed her small wrist and yanked her out the chair.

The patrons of the restaurant screamed in panic while Ashley screamed in pain. William heard none of it. The pounding of his heart was the only thing he could hear.

"WILLIAM!! PLEASE STOP!!!" Ashley screamed as he effortlessly dragged her to the car as if she were a rag doll. He picked her up and threw her inside of his Flying Spur as if she were trash.

"What have I done? What have I gotten myself into?" Ashley asked herself silently.

Many years ago, her mother told her that being nosy would get her in trouble someday. She could see now that her mother's prediction was true.

She tried to speak to him, but William had mentally checked out. The only thing that he could focus on as he drove to his parents' affluent neighborhood were the images running through his head.

Ashley gasped as they drove down the paved road to the large mansion. She had visited their home in the daytime. But the nighttime lights illuminated the house in such a way that made the home seem majestic. As she turned to look at William, she screamed. He was driving, but his head was turned to the right, staring directly at her.

This was a scene straight out of a horror story. Never in her life had she ever witnessed anything so sinister. She couldn't understand how he was driving, staying in his lane, and handling the curves in the road while staring directly at her.

"Wi...Will? What's wrong? Are you-"

"Let's go!" William said angrily as he expertly stopped the car and opened the car door.

For the first time ever, Ashley was truly afraid of the man she slept beside every night. Her intuition told her to hop in the driver's seat and drive off. But her fear kept her rooted in the passenger seat. He swung the passenger door open with so much force that the car shook.

"I said let's go!"

"William, I'm so sorry. Let's forget about this whole thing. I just want to go home," Ashley cried.

"Oh, now you want to go home. Why is that? Weren't you just here? Since you wanted to meet them, let's go inside." William said as he pulled her out of the seat and up to the entrance of the home.

The moment William placed his key in the lock and opened the door, Ashley knew something was seriously wrong. The interior did not match the outside of the home at all. The rancid odor made bile rise in her throat. She tried to turn and run, but the grip that he had on her wrist felt like a vice grip.

"I said let's go," William said. "Mommy. Daddy. I'm home," he said in a singsong voice that did not match his demeanor.

"He's crazy," Ashley thought as she trembled.

Fear, as well as the horrible odor that seemed to intensify as they walked deeper into the home, had stolen her voice.

"Mom. Dad. This is Ashley. Ashley, meet the parents," William said, as he pushed open the large bedroom door.

Ashley screamed out in terror as she tried to run out the door. But William wasn't having it. He dragged her to the two emaciated people chained to the wall like animals. They sat in what appeared to be years of their own filth. Ashley tried to break free, but William possessed the strength of a madman and letting her go was out of the question.

"This piece of shit is my father, the so-called Dr. Norman Hugo. Say hello, Daddy."

The man looked at Ashley somberly with his sunken eyes. He murmured something behind the strap that covered his mouth as if he were pleading for help. Ashley couldn't make out what he was saying, nor did she want to. She continued to scream as she tried to break free.

"Why are you screaming? This is what you wanted to see, right?" William asked with a crazed look in his eyes.

"William, I'm sorry. Please just let me go. I won't say anything. William. I-"

Ashley's sentence halted the moment she turned around and saw the video that was playing on the old box television. She couldn't make sense of what she was watching. It was her. No, it wasn't her. It was her mother. In the video, Sharon appeared to be in her early thirties. Ashley could see who she assumed was Dr. Norman Hugo, her mother, and what appeared to be either a sixteen- or seventeen-year-old William.

Ashley gasped. Tears filled her eyes as she watched the horrific things her mother was doing to her soon-to-be husband. She had no idea that they even knew each other. But most importantly, she also simply couldn't understand why her mother was performing sexual acts on what was clearly a child.

"Now you know the truth. The wealthiest people hide their secrets behind beautiful things so their dirty insides won't be suspected," William admitted.

Tears ran down Ashley's face. She wanted to look away, but she simply couldn't. The pain that she was feeling was crippling.

"When I was growing up, my piece of shit father, held these things called '*experiments*', which were nothing more than him making people do sexual acts for money. He hid behind the title of doctor, but my father was never a doctor. He never finished high school or went to college. That's why you couldn't find him when you looked online. He had money from an old trust fund and from selling his 'experiment' videos. The subjects were women, mainly prostitutes or single mothers,"

Ashley's head snapped back at the sentence. Her dad was lazy as fuck, but he was still her mother's husband. She was not single. At the realization of her own thoughts, Ashley gagged.

"That's right, Your mother was and still is a whore. My father found her working at a brothel and offered her a job as a housekeeper. He then offered her me. I was two weeks short of being seventeen in that video, and Sharon did things to me that I wasn't ready for. I was completely under her spell. My so-called mother ignored everything just so she could continue to live the way she was living.

But Sharon. Sharon lied to everyone, even you. Ashton wasn't your father. She drained the life out of him with her promiscuous ways then had him murdered. I have a video of that too," William said happily. It brought him joy to tell the truth about Sharon.

"I don't understand," Ashley cried.

This was too much for her. She had no idea that she would discover so much from wanting to meet her in-laws. She couldn't think, and William's loud murmurs were making it harder to focus. Anger made her snatch the tape off the mouth of the nearest person next to her.

Tammy tried to scream, but she didn't have the strength to do so. Her voice came out no louder than a whisper. For the past decade, William had fed them only once a day. Only giving them enough to keep them alive.

"I'm sorry, Son. I didn't know what to do," his mother said weakly.

"Shut up your lies!!" William said as he slapped his mother so hard that a few of her rotten teeth flew across the filthy room.

His father murmured loudly but the gag in his mouth was preventing his words from coming out.

"Why don't you remove that gag so I can hear what he's saying?" William said with a crazed sinister grin. He pushed Ashley towards his father with so much force that she nearly fell in a pile of waste.

With trembling hands, she removed the gag in sheer confusion. She was so stunned that it took her a while to calculate what she was seeing.

Looking between Normans' legs, she saw that his genitalia were missing. Between his legs was as smooth as a Ken doll. If she hadn't known any better, she would've assumed that he was born that way. William's plastic surgery skills were truly top tier. Placing her shock aside, Ashley looked at the gag in her hand and saw that William had turned the severed penis into what appeared to be a pacifier.

Once the pieces fit together in her head, Ashley screamed before passing out.

William smirked. "Hope you're happy since I let you meet the parents."

Identity Crisis

Keira N. James

Copyright

Chapter One

Storming across the vacant parking lot, Ember brainstormed her defense for premeditated murder. The rubber heels of her combat boots stomped aggressively against the pavement as ominous grey clouds gathered in the evening sky—overcast.

Steadily, rain began to fall. Ember rushed into battle with the harsh meteorological conditions while her mind swirled with a gamut of emotions. However, one feeling presented itself front and center.

Pure unadulterated hate.

Anxiety riddled her insides, prompting her to readjust the Nike backpack on her back. The contents of the bag included a folded sheet of paper inked with a disheartening diagnosis. The results were known only to herself and her gynecologist, and as she continued with purposeful strides to confront her ex-lover, Quentin, she feared all she stood to lose once she shared the news with her fiancé, Kendall.

Earlier in the afternoon, during what was supposed to be a routine doctor's visit, Ember was served a dose of reality that ushered her into the cold arms of sterility.

For months, a sexually transmitted disease lay dormant in her body. She remained asymptomatic, and because there were no signs or symptoms, she was unaware of the need to be treated. Due to her lack of knowledge, Ember was now a barren woman with a scarred uterus and a void that could only be filled with vengeance.

"I'm gonna kill that motherfucker!" she threatened, jogging out of the downpour of rain.

Ember tossed the hood over her chestnut brown tresses and then burst through the glass doors of the high-rise building. Heading straight for the elevators, she repeatedly stabbed the round button labeled '15' until the doors eased closed.

In the corner, she stood chin to chest to conceal her identity from the poorly hidden cameras. Her weight shifted from one foot to the other as she struggled to decide which emotion to tackle first.

She was hurt, angry, disappointed, and confused.

Her fragile mental state couldn't be described in just one word. In fact, she wasn't even sure if Webster could define it.

While the elevator took its precious time ascending, Ember fiddled absentmindedly with the two-carat solitaire diamond on her left finger. The flawless gem was given to her by the one she loved the most. With Kendall at the forefront of her mind, she reached into her backpack and fished out her cell phone.

Kendall: Babe, we need to talk.

A film of sweat coated her palm after reading the message. Suddenly, the thought of coming clean frightened her, so she pocketed the device and took on a vow of silence, choosing not to respond. Instead, she tortured herself by thinking about all the light Kendall brought to her life and how undeserving she was of the destruction brought upon their union.

Ember's relationship meant everything to her, but foolishly, she risked it all for a man who promised her the world, only to leave the weight of it on her shoulders. And for that, she was filled with more regret than sand on a beach.

Leaning against the wall, Ember tucked a damp lock of hair behind her ear. She was somewhat relieved that her fiancée hadn't called. The lapse in communication prolonged the moment of breaking Ken's heart. And though she knew the time would soon come, she stuffed the thought in the back of her mind and focused on the task at hand.

Buzz. Buzz. Buzz.

Heart pounding, Ember pushed off the elevator wall. She reached into the bag, careful not to pull out her gun, and retrieved her phone. Without looking at the screen she assumed it to be Kendall. A nervous breath fled her nostrils as she used biometrics to unlock the device.

Oh, fuck me! She thought.

Ironically, the notification was an alert from the Flow app. It informed her that she was due to start ovulating the next day. Seeing the words on the calendar was enough to make her cry a river because having a baby had been the topic of discussion in her household for the past year. Now, because of her betrayal, there was a different conversation to be had; one that included telling the love of her life that she could no longer carry their children.

Ding!

Heavy-heartedly, Ember uninstalled the Flow application and placed the phone in her backpack just as the elevator came to a stop. From her back pocket, she grabbed the fake ID badge required for entry and stepped off the lift. The moment she did, darkness engulfed her.

Chapter Two

I know he's here.

During the day, Legacy Branding Company bustled with staff and clients, but it was currently after-hours, leaving the building empty and quiet. Despite it being a Friday evening, she knew Quentin would be in his corner office because of his overachieving nature.

Ember stomped down the carpeted halls noting how the storm mirrored her mood. The resounding rolls of thunder symbolized her pounding heart, and the constant fall of heavy rain represented the tears of every child she would never conceive naturally, every kick she'd never feel in her stomach, and every gene she'd never pass on to the baby girl they desperately wanted.

So badly, she wished the rain could wash away her problems as easily as it washed away the dirt from the streets, but she was fully aware that life didn't work that way. Life was unpredictable and cruel as fuck.

"How could I have been so stupid?" she questioned, while marching towards Quentin's office.

The absence of overhead lighting made the journey a challenging one, but she had ambled through the maze of hallways enough times to have the layout committed to memory.

Turn by turn, Ember closed the distance with heat radiating from her body in waves. She had every intention of bursting through Quentin's door with guns blazing, but when his office came into view, a faint voice in the back of her head suggested she be patient.

As a Navy vet, she was taught to trust her instincts, and at the moment, that's exactly what she did.

Scaling the wall sideways, she crept towards the door with anxiety tracing her subtle curves. Her heart raced at the thought of what she'd find, and seconds later, curiosity killed her proverbial cat.

"Well, well, well. What do we have here?" Ember mumbled tauntingly.

On the opposite side of the wooden barrier, unmistakable cries of ecstasy reverberated. The sexual sounds piqued her interest as she inched closer and peered over the portion of the frosted glass door.

"Stick your tongue out and relax your throat," Quentin coached.

On her tiptoes, Ember watched as he grabbed either side of a woman's head and pumped his gonorrhea-ridden pipe down her throat. Ember couldn't see the woman's face, but she vividly remembered being in the same position many times before. Now, however, she fought the urge to throw up in her mouth at the thought of his dick being anywhere near her.

"Ugh!" She protested silently, rolling her eyes.

Seeing Quentin defile another woman didn't incite one ounce of jealousy because she knew she wasn't his only mistress. However, what she lacked in jealousy, she more than made up for in pettiness.

Quentin ruined her life the minute he used her loneliness to his advantage, so she believed it was only fair for her to return the favor.

I got something for your ass, you dirty dick bastard.

Ember knew how much Quentin valued discretion, especially since he was married and the CEO of the most esteemed marketing firm in The South, but any and all respect she had for him was gone after he ruined her chances of becoming a mother.

Quickly grabbing her phone, she began to film his raunchy sexcapade, intending to send the final cut to his wife and the local media. He stood to lose so much from the scandal and Ember couldn't wait to witness his downfall.

Stepping to the left, Ember angled the phone to get a better view. Just as the fornicators switched positions, an orange and black butterfly tattoo came into her line of vision, leaving the world spinning lazily around her.

Chapter Three

What the fuck?

An inability to sustain her own weight forced Ember into a codependent relationship with the wall. As she reached back and held it for support, the most important organ in her body fought fiercely for its freedom, sending her respirations near the brink of tachycardia.

Several minutes had passed before she fully understood the enormity of deceit unfolding right before her eyes. Ember's uterus may have been impaired, but her vision was impeccable. There was no denying that the woman Quentin had bent over his desk was the same woman she was set to marry next year. She recognized the tattoo on her left shoulder, deeming it unnecessary to see the face she loved waking up to.

Her heart blackened with vengeance. Vines of retribution wrapped themselves around it.

As she reached into the bag and grabbed the grip of a Ruger LC9S, she held back tears that threatened to spill down her cheeks.

Hastily, Ember flipped the lever off of 'safety' and pulled back the slide in one swift motion. She'd done it so many times during her tour in Kuwait that it was like second nature.

Without a second thought, she pointed, aimed, and emptied the clip, employing all eight rounds of the magazine.

The glass shattered upon impact. Tiny shards impaled her tear-stained face. After the gun clicked, her clammy hands failed to bear the weight of the pistol, sending it falling to the floor with a hard thud, along with the two bodies in front of her.

The magnitude of what she'd done came crashing down swiftly and heavily. Her heart raced against time as she stood as still as the night, scoping the bloody scene with the blue eyes inherited from her mother's recessive gene.

The military hardened her to the point of being desensitized to violence, but Ember was uncertain if she'd ever recover from what she'd just done because although she had shot down many a man during her time in battle, she never thought someone she loved would ever be on the receiving end of her gun.

One thing she was sure of though, her actions may have been impulsive, but she didn't regret it one bit.

No one fucked her over and lived to talk about it.

Lazily, she leaned to retrieve the fallen weapon and stuff it in her bag. She then entered the office with a pungent scent attacking her nostrils. She pinched her nose and stepped over the bodies, carefully avoiding the puddles of blood, and looking at her treacherous lover who lay face-down on the carpet.

One by one, Ember picked up eight spent shells while disappointment and despair manifested into a lump in her throat. She gagged and dry heaved several times before swallowing her feelings. She prolonged her breakdown because now wasn't the time to be thrown off her game with emotions. She needed to focus because attention to detail was of the utmost importance and any little mistake could be a costly one.

With one last scan over the office, Ember retraced her steps and exited the space. In her haste to flee the crime scene, she failed to notice an eyewitness hiding under a nearby desk.

Chapter Four

Zipping through the maze of cubicles like a lab rat on steroids, Ember fled the scene. She rifled through her backpack for a burner phone filled with the contacts of old shipmates.

The impulsive decision to kill two bitches with eight bullets left her mind in a ball of confusion, and while she didn't make it a habit to murder civilians in cold blood, she refused to let Quentin and Kendall's transgressions go unpunished.

As she texted an old battle buddy for assistance with handling the bodies, she recalled the days of her job as a Special Warfare Combatant-Craft Crewman. It entailed neutralizing anyone who threatened the security of the nation, but something about this particular kill felt different.

It felt...troubling.

Ember couldn't put her finger on it, but there was an unsettling force holding her resolve captive, and to add insult to injury, a Google alert came to her main line, reminding her of the upcoming arrival of Mercury's retrograde.

She grew increasingly anxious because, among all the madness, the last thing she needed was to worry about an optical illusion causing chaos and major disruptions. There were so many loose ends to tie up in a short amount of time; she couldn't afford any distractions beyond her control.

Dumb ass retrograde.

Against her better judgment, Ember silenced the annoying voice and sent the message to her old pal, Kaine St. James.

The two served in the military together before Kaine went AWOL after killing multiple shipmates in a fit of rage. Shortly after her friend's desertion, Ember was dishonorably discharged for failing a psychiatric evaluation after her last tour in Kuwait.

These days, the battle buddies moonlighted as hitwomen for an exclusive black-market network called 'The Underground'. Usually, Ember was cleaner and more calculated with her kills, but today, emotions overshadowed logic, and now more than ever, she needed a friend to help clean up the mess she'd made.

Click!

Click!

Click!

The ex-militant halted mid-stride. With her heart pounding intensely in her chest, she turned slowly, lowering her doe eyes into a squint.

"Who's there?" she tossed into the darkness. Waiting impatiently, the rookie detective listened for a response but saw nothing and heard no one. Her eyes darted hastily, visually investigating the source of the noise, but after several seconds of nothing, she defiantly shook off the bad vibes again. Walking away, Ember replied to a cryptic text message from Kaine.

Click!

Click!

Click!

Three steps into her stride, the same unidentified sound put her on high alert. She expected no other staff members to be at work on a Friday evening, but unbeknownst to her, she was sadly mistaken.

Craning her neck from left to right, Ember searched high and low but came up empty. Still, she tucked the burner away and reloaded her pistol in seconds. She couldn't afford to have someone attest to her crime, so she was fully prepared to commit it again.

"If there's somebody here, you better show yourselves now!" she warned.

Creeping in the opposite direction of where she was headed, Ember padded through the unlit area, peeking into every cubicle with her gun leading the way. She briefly scanned each one to her satisfaction but noted nothing out of the ordinary.

Stealthily, she sidestepped further down the narrow passageway until she walked upon a desk with the computer screen illuminated. The monitor displayed a slideshow of a beautiful sandy-haired woman and a toddler with coils of the same color. The child couldn't have been any older than two years old, but what struck Ember as odd was the little girl's slightly slanted eyes and dimpled chin. Her adorable little face was vaguely familiar, but for the life of her, she couldn't place where she knew it from.

Sadly, the distraction of imagining what her own little girl would look like diminished her situational awareness, and Ember's failure to thoroughly check the desk was an oversight she'd soon pay for.

The desk belonged to the woman currently hiding underneath it. Her name was Hazel Cromer, and she was an enemy Ember didn't know she had.

Chapter Five

"Shit!" Hazel thought, clutching her camera tightly against her. Knees to chest, she sat as still as the Statue of David with her lungs begging to drink in a deep breath of air.

Hazel was Quentin's second assistant and another one of his mistresses. She became scorned after learning of his ongoing affair with Ember, and though she recognized that they both were wrong for coveting another woman's husband, Hazel made the mistake of assuming she was the only one on the side.

One evening when she found them engrossed in the throes of passion, she swore to somehow, someway, avenge her broken heart, but she had no idea her enemy would be the one to beat her to the punch.

Holding her breath, she sat motionless under the desk with fear and trembling. She didn't know the woman in Quentin's office, but what she did know was that every Friday at seven p.m. for the past eight weeks, Ember waltzed into Quentin's office for an evening quickie.

Since she learned of their secret sex sessions, Hazel had been waiting to advance her personal agenda, which entailed using the photos to extort money from Quentin to help raise the daughter he didn't know they shared.

However, hearing gunshots was enough to deter her. The most action she anticipated was a screaming match and maybe a hand or two being thrown. In no way did she expect to witness a double homicide.

Squeezing her eyes closed, Hazel prayed a silent prayer that Ember wouldn't notice her. Seconds later, she opened them to find a pair of black combat boots standing inches away from her.

Oh, God. Oh, God.

She cupped a hand over her mouth and breathed unsteadily through her nose. Tears flowed freely at the thought of being the third casualty. With regret, she risked her life by trying to be vindictive, and at this point, she knew her plan wasn't worth the trouble.

Lord, please. I don't wanna die like this.

Hazel was only twenty-four years old and had her whole life ahead of her. The last thing she wanted was to leave her baby girl, Abbygail, alone in the world, especially over a man who cared nothing for either of them.

THUMP!

The murder weapon fell to the floor, landing near Hazel's feet. Her reflexes went into overdrive after being so close to the cold piece of deadly steel. She'd never been so close to a gun before, so she retracted her hand so hard and fast; her head bumped against the desk, interrupting the silence.

Shit!

Ember picked up the gun in a hurry while simultaneously yanking at the desk chair. Her movements were so violent that the chair knocked against Hazel's leg.

Always the observant one, she noticed the chair's resistance. Swiftly, she pulled the chair back, sending it crashing into the desk behind her.

"If there's someone under here, I'm giving you 'til the count of one to reveal yourself," Ember warned with the gun ready to fire.

Hazel contemplated her surrender with tears flowing rapidly down her face. Soft cries gathered in her throat and demanded to be released. It took all the willpower she could muster to remain as still and quiet as possible when she heard the gun cock.

"One," Ember counted.

Eyes clenched, Hazel prayed for the safety of her daughter when Ember leaned to check under the desk. A deafening clap of thunder rumbled, followed by the buzzing of an electronic device.

"I knew she'd come through," Ember spoke as she stood upright.

Under the desk, Hazel cautiously cracked open her left eye. It wasn't until the mortal Grim Reaper began conversing on the phone that she realized God had sent her a lifeline.

Oh, thank you, Jesus! she mouthed.

Hazel breathed a silent sigh of relief at the sight of Ember's feet moving further in the distance. The phone call she received took place a millisecond before she was discovered under the desk, and for that, the damsel in distress was thankful.

When the door to the stairwell slammed, Hazel scrambled from under the desk, visibly shaken but relieved at the same time.

She paced the floor like a madwoman and ran a trembling hand through her natural curls. As she contemplated her next move, she considered two options.

One—she could go home to her baby girl and suppress any and all memories of the night and do nothing. Two—she could take advantage of the opportunity and leverage the situation for her financial gain.

What should I do? Hazel questioned in deep thought.

Blackmailing Ember was not only for avenging her broken heart but also for providing for her disabled child. Her salary at Legacy Branding was decent, but the care and medication required for her daughter's disability were ridiculously expensive. Now that an opportunity had presented itself to lighten the load, there were some decisions to be made.

Hazel continued pacing and weighing her options, not thinking too deeply about all the things that could go wrong. "Fuck it," she finally declared, choosing to enact the reckless, ill-thought-out plan.

Grabbing the nearest desk chair, the extortionist sat at the computer. As she logged into her Google Drive account, she worked quickly to upload the pictures to an external hard drive.

After everything she'd witnessed, she felt her silence came with a price, and the only question she had to answer now was how much it was worth.

To Hazel's detriment, Ember had doubled back to wait for Kaine to arrive. Quietly, she backpedaled out of sight and hugged the corner, sneaking glances at the sandy-haired woman from the computer screen.

She watched Hazel upload photos of her in various stages of her crime and it seared all seven trillion of her nerve endings. Ember didn't know this woman from a can of paint, but she found relief in the woman's ignorance. While Hazel prepped her case for blackmail and extortion, she didn't realize how quickly the predator had become the prey.

From a distance, Ember observed Hazel tapping away on the keyboard. The blackmailing bitch was drafting a document and at that moment, Ember thought quickly on her feet and sent another text message to Kaine letting her know their plans had changed.

Chapter Six

Careful not to alarm her new nemesis, Ember backpedaled to the stairwell until the wall obstructed Hazel from view. Out of sight, she fumbled through her bag and grabbed a pen to hold the door open.

After securing her reentry, Ember hurriedly shuffled down fifteen flights of stairs. On her descent she scolded herself for the major oversight. Had she not returned to Quentin's office, she never would've caught Hazel plotting the downfall she deserved.

Ember couldn't have been more thankful for Kaine suggesting she stay and help with staging the scene, and for that, she'd always be indebted to her friend.

Pushing through the stairwell door, Ember's chest deflated with relief after laying eyes on Kaine, who'd entered the building through the service entryway. Kaine still looked the same with her flawless skin and strikingly sharp facial features. However, that was something Ember would be remiss not to point out.

"Nice leg," she joked, pointing at Kaine's prosthetic.

Facetiously, Kaine thanked her before turning from side to side to give her a good look. She lost her limb during a military training exercise that was deemed an accident, but Kaine found out that the 'accident' was deliberate and handled the situation accordingly.

"Now that we have that out of the way, let's take care of this bitch. We can catch up when we're done here," Kaine asserted, wasting no time pushing past Ember.

Ascending the stairs, Kaine carried a black duffle bag that matched her all-black ensemble. Ember didn't have to ask about the contents of the bag because she knew her girl was thorough and had everything they needed.

"So, what was your plan coming into this?" Kaine asked out of curiosity. She knew Ember wasn't as sloppy or impulsive as she had been tonight, so she was interested in her explanation.

"Honestly, I was just gonna shoot his dick off and mail it to him, but when I saw him banging Kendall's back out, I just fuckin' lost it."

"That's reasonable," Kaine offered, shrugging with understanding.

Taking the last step, Ember put a finger to her lips. She removed the pen from the door and cracked it open further. Leaning in, both women listened for anything forewarning them that the mystery woman was still in place.

The click-clacking of keys on the keyboard put them on notice and prompted Kaine to pull a few items out of the bag.

"I knew you'd come through for me, Sis."

"Like only I can," Kaine replied, keeping an eye out.

Ember thanked her quietly as she grabbed the Nike sneakers, an Albany State University sweatshirt, and jeans to go under the set of black Dickies coveralls.

When Ember realized there was a snitch in the mix her mind immediately computed different ways to exonerate herself. This included changing her clothes and planting Hazel's DNA in the office. She had no intentions of killing anyone before confronting Quentin, so she didn't come prepared. And because she didn't have time to leave and grab all the necessities herself, she tapped into a deadly and invaluable resource.

After changing in record time, Ember zipped up the coveralls and tossed her old clothes in Kaine's duffle bag to burn later. Kaine slipped on a pair of latex gloves, and with synchronicity, the pair took deep breaths and mentally prepared to fulfill their duty.

Together, they snuck onto the work floor and scurried to their perspective corners. With Ember crouched behind a nearby cubicle, and Kaine tucked in a corner near the elevators, Hazel was stuck between two assassins and a hard place—a dangerous place to be.

The deadly duo watched as Hazel walked to the printer and grabbed a letter. Kaine eyed Ember from across the way, seeking the command to move in, but Ember shook her head, signaling her to stand down.

Hazel trotted back to the desk and quickly packed up her belongings before hurrying for the elevators. When she reached the walkway that offered a line of vision into Quentin's office, she stood and drank in the gruesome scene. Clothes were sprawled everywhere. Blood and glass littered the floor, and despite her weak stomach, she couldn't look away.

Leaving two dead bodies in the office left her conflicted, but she hushed her conscience and deemed them deserving of what happened to them.

Praying they rotted in hell, Hazel turned to walk away, feeling surer of herself than she should've been. She was oblivious to the danger lurking around the corner, and it showed on her face when Ember rose from the shadows like a Phoenix from the ashes and asked, "Going somewhere?"

Chapter Seven

A hard gasp of surprise escaped Hazel's plump lips. Her parasympathetic nervous system pressured her to take flight, but terror knotted inside of her and held her body hostage.

"I asked you a question," Ember pressed, closing the space between them. Hazel willed her feet to move, but fear paralyzed her. While she stood frozen in place she realized the grave mistake she'd made. Her only option now was to make like a Boeing jet and take flight.

Hazel made a run for it and sidestepped Ember, leaving a trail of her belongings behind. Ember tilted her head slightly to the left and watched in amusement, knowing that the little rat wouldn't get far. While Hazel dashed towards the elevator, the aggressor stood in place and counted down.

"5...4...3...2...1."

On cue, Kaine stepped into view and used Hazel's momentum to her advantage. With force, Kaine pushed her into the wall then grabbed the collar of her button up and yanked her to the floor. Using her weight, Kaine pinned Hazel down. As Hazel made vain attempts to wiggle her way to freedom, Ember retrieved a small bottle from the side pocket of her coveralls and poured a liberal amount of poisonous liquid onto the cloth.

Hazel yelled and craned her neck to avoid Ember but to no avail. Ember placed the cloth over her nose and mouth and the more Hazel screamed and gasped, the more toxins she ingested. Seconds later, her movement ceased.

"Which way?" Kaine asked, climbing off the unconscious body.

"That way." Ember directed Kaine with a head nod as she grabbed Hazel's feet. Together, they carried her to Quentin's office, careful not to leave a trail of their DNA. When they reached the workspace, Ember made a conscious decision not to look at the face of either of the traitors. Seeing Kendall naked and face down was not the way she wanted to remember her; however, Ember's efforts were unsuccessful.

She glanced at the back of her beloved's head, zeroing in on the bullet wound. The bullet wound she was responsible for. At the sight, she dropped Hazel's feet, leaving Kaine to bear the load. She couldn't take her eyes off the catastrophe, nor shake the feeling that something felt off.

Absent-mindedly, she backed into the corner, sliding down the wall with tears doing the same on her face. Saliva rapidly invaded her mouth like the soldiers in Normandy, and it wasn't long before her lunch took a one-way trip up her esophagus.

"Awk!" Ember dry heaved.

Kaine dropped Hazel's top half and rushed to her friend's aid. With sympathetic eyes and a calming tone, she advised Ember, "I know this hurts, but I need you to hold it together."

Ember took heed to her friend's advice and forced the bitterness down with a hard swallow. As much as she wanted to release it all, she knew that doing so would incriminate her. She couldn't afford to have her DNA anywhere in the room.

"If this is too much, I can call Ace to help me finish."

"I'm good," Ember fibbed, not wanting Kaine to involve her boyfriend.

She was anything but okay, but she figured if she said it out loud, the lie would somehow manifest into the truth.

"Okay. Let's make this quick," Kaine advised.

As a team, the hitwomen painted Hazel as a lover scorned. They started by planting her fingerprints on the gun, knocking pictures off the wall and whatnots off the desk, then moved on to using her hands to scratch Quentin's neck to get his DNA under her nails to show signs of a struggle. Lastly, they banged Hazel's head against the floor, making it appear as though she passed out from blunt force trauma.

Neither of the vets worried about a toxicology report showing traces of chloroform because they knew it didn't stay in a person's system very long, so by the time Hazel came to and her accusations were fact-checked by the police, the poison would be long gone from her bloodstream.

Carefully stepping around the blood and bodies, Ember and Kaine stood back, checking out their handiwork. They were satisfied with how well it worked out in such a short amount of time because normally in their line of work, there was a lot of planning and preparation for things as such. However, the amount of experience and knowledge they gained in the military was very useful when it came to improvising.

"Do you want a minute alone with her?" Kaine asked, looking at her friend.

"Yeah, can you give me a second?"

Kaine knew firsthand how it felt to see a loved one lie lifeless on the floor. Three years ago, she watched her Nana get gunned down in her own home and the sense of guilt and helplessness she felt was something she had yet to get over.

"Say no more," Kaine stated with understanding. She gave Ember a tight hug before leaving the room to do a sweep of the rest of the floor, ensuring there were no more potential witnesses among them.

As Ember studied the curvaceous naked body, she reflected on her and Kendall's relationship. It was a cold and rainy Wednesday afternoon. Kendall was stretched out unconscious on the side of the road after being beaten by her boyfriend. Ember just so happened to be driving by and stopped to help.

She nursed Kendall back to health and they continued to spend more and more time together. Eventually, they fell in love. From then on, the two were inseparable until Kendall was promoted.

After being spoiled by the time and attention she'd gotten over the months, Ember struggled with Ken's new hectic schedule and sought solace in the arms of another. By the time Kendall realized there was a strain on their relationship and attempted to fix it, Ember was too far gone to stop her scandalous love affair.

A strong wind seeped through the bullet hole in the window, sending a putrid smell up Ember's nostrils. The scent ushered her from the stroll down memory lane and she was thankful for the distraction. She gave the room one last glance before walking out.

When she found Kaine leaning against the wall eyeing her with pity, she removed the coveralls and straightened her posture while tucking the ID badge into her back pocket. "Did you make the call?" Ember asked, taking the focus off her.

"I did, and we have about five minutes to get the hell out of here before this place is swarming with cops, and we both know, I don't need those problems," she said, referring to her status as a deserter from the Navy.

"Shit, me either. Kendall was a fuckin' detective!" Ember confessed.

Chapter Eight

Rushing, the assassins gathered their belongings and ventured towards the stairwell. With three minutes to spare, Kaine and Ember rushed out of the building, each going their separate ways. Thankfully, the storm showed them a little mercy and eased up enough to allow for a swift getaway.

Puddles splashed under Ember's feet as she widened her strides and ran to her black Jeep Cherokee. She yanked open the back door, tossed the backpack in, and shuffled to the driver's seat. Once in, she brought the car to life and burned rubber out of the parking lot.

A smokey haze blanketed the city until blinding red, white, and blue lights penetrated the fog. The intermittent lights instilled fear in Ember's heart as it raced against time. As she traveled through the night, her eyes averted between the road and the rearview mirror until a fleet of cruisers and ambulances turned into the parking lot.

"Fuck!" She cursed, banging a hand against the steering wheel. Though she and Kaine were confident in their scheme, Ember couldn't shake the nagging feeling in her gut. She wasn't sure what her intuition was trying to tell her, but she knew that focusing on the unknown would only increase her anxiety, so she put her attention solely on the road and expertly navigated the slick terrain of Macon, Georgia's back streets.

Drifting onto a side street, Ember entered Fort Hawkins's neighborhood. The crime-infested area was littered with abandoned houses, dope fiends, and D-boys. The speed bumps kept her at a steady pace as she passed through with a pesky conscience trying to convince her that killing Kendall and Quentin was unnecessary.

At that moment, part of her began to feel guilty. She considered that her reaction was dramatic, but just as quickly as she became remorseful, she also justified her actions by reminding herself that the military had bred her to be a stone-cold killer for over fourteen years. Neutralizing threats had been embedded into her, but what Ember forgot to remember was that her actions as a civilian came with consequences.

Turning out of the neighborhood, Ember slipped into the groove of oncoming traffic. She put the pedal to the metal, weaving in and out of lanes until her east side townhome was in view.

She pulled into the driveway and sat, willing herself to interpret the telepathic message from her intuition. Laying her pounding head against the headrest, Ember ran a hand down her face, not believing her reality.

As her thoughts raced, one in particular came rushing back like the waves of a typhoon. She raised her head and cursed herself for forgetting one important piece of an already complex puzzle.

"Shit! I forgot to grab the fuckin' flash drive."

Chapter Nine

Darkness faded into light as Hazel slowly regained consciousness. The metallic scent of blood invited itself into her nostrils and triggered a not-so-distant memory.

Suddenly, her eyes bulged with panic. She sat up and scanned the room with terror and disbelief distorting her mind. When she noticed a gun lying next to the right of her, her heart pounded like the bassline of a rugged hip-hop beat.

Gradually, Hazel began putting together pieces of a deceitful puzzle. The realization that she'd been set up began to sink in and it incited the only emotion stronger than hope. It incited fear.

Unrelenting fear.

Anxiety and dread tormented her on their own accord before she screamed from the depths of her blackened soul. Needing to get away, Hazel scrambled; however, the crimson liquid leaking from Quentin's head had pooled around him and created a makeshift Slip 'N Slide.

She struggled to stand firmly and after three failed attempts, she crawled to the door. On the threshold, she used the wall for support and pulled herself up. She took a step towards the exit but stopped when she realized the murderers who'd set her up could've still been in the building.

For her own protection, she maneuvered around the bodies and blood and picked up the gun. She had never used one before but there was a first time for everything, and this time was a life and death situation.

Just as Hazel attempted to exit the office, she came face to face with the last person she expected to see.

"Freeze!" the cop instructed.

Shocked and fearing for her life, Hazel flinched and mistakenly pulled the trigger. After the shot rang out, the remaining officers opened fire and killed her instantly.

Chapter Ten

Ember's breaths came in ragged gasps as she sat in the garage scolding herself for being so sloppy and distracted by emotions. The neighborhood was shrouded in an eerie silence, broken only by the sudden buzzing of her burner phone.

"Kaine, I forgot--" she started as soon as she answered.

"I got it and destroyed it. We're good."

"Thank you!" Ember said through a breath of relief. The line went dead with a click, signaling the end of the call and the business with her and Kaine.

She didn't know when or how her shipmate managed to get the drive, but Ember was grateful that Kaine had looked out for her during her time of emotional duress.

With the worry of the flash drive out of her head, she rounded up her belongings. With cautious steps, Ember slipped from the safety of the car. The gravel crunched beneath her boots and each sound magnified to a deafening roar in the stillness of the night. Watching her six, she backpedaled to the door and shuffled into her townhome. The moment she crossed the threshold, her intuition blared with warnings.

Every shadow appeared larger, and every creak of the floors sounded like an indication of impending doom.

As a precaution, she reached into the backpack and grabbed hold of her gun. She clutched the cold metal with her fingers trembling with anticipation and fear. With cautious and strategic steps, she tiptoed further into the minimally illuminated living room, leaving the front door cracked in case she needed to make a quick escape.

Murdering two people in cold blood left Ember paranoid; and paranoia left her more insecure than she had ever been. Truthfully, she didn't know for certain if anyone was actually in the home, but she knew it was better to be safe than sorry.

As she approached the kitchen, her pulse quickened with a mounting sense of dread. Every flicker of movement felt like a potential threat lurking in the darkness. A silent prayer sat on her lips as she rounded the corner moving through the dimly lit room like a shadow. Her movements were fluid and silent as she checked each corner for any sign of intrusion.

So far, the house lay empty. The walls echoed with abandonment. No sinister figures were lurking in the shadows and no apparent threats as far as her eye could see.

With the bottom level of the home clear, relief flooded Ember like a tidal wave, washing away the suffocating weight of fear that threatened to consume her. She allowed herself a moment of rest, physically and mentally. Her breaths came in shaky gasps as she leaned against the granite island in exhaustion. But even as she closed her eyes and welcomed relief, the presence of doubt lingered on the edges of her consciousness. It silently reminded her of a truth she dared not confess to anyone and one she never wanted to face again.

It wasn't until she heard a soft patter in the distance that Ember's eyes snapped open. Her heart leaped into her throat with a sudden rush of adrenaline. Hastily, she pushed off the island in one fluid motion with the pistol clenched tightly in her trembling grasp.

Moving towards the source of the sound, she found it to be coming from upstairs. One by one, she ascended them with a weapon leading the way.

Hypervigilant, she rushed into the guest bedroom, pointing the barrel of the pistol toward every corner before moving to the closet. She tossed aside clothes and shoes but nothing or no one presented itself.

Slowly, she backed out of the room and headed for the ensuite. The closer she stepped, the louder the patter became. With a steadying breath, Ember walked inside the room to find the bathroom door slightly ajar with steam pouring outside.

She crept closer and pulled open the door. Her gaze swept over the figure standing beneath the spray of water. "Kendall?" she breathed.

Disbelief laced her voice as she took in the sight before her. Her fiancée, whom she thought she'd killed, turned towards her with fearful eyes. Ember's expression was a mixture of confusion and concern. It felt like she was in a twilight zone, and nothing was as it seemed.

"Ember?" Kendall said shakily, her voice tinged with fear. "Why are you pointing a gun at me?"

Ember's hand shook as she lowered the gun. "I... I thought... I thought I..." Her words faltered; the truth too bitter to speak aloud.

Returning to her shower after realizing she wasn't in danger, Kendall said, "Put that thing away, babe. You're just paranoid again. I told you; you need to talk to someone about that. That's why I messaged you today saying we needed to talk.

Kandice just got a job as an industrial psychologist at that fancy marketing company downtown. I think it's called Legacy Branding or something. Anyway, I was hoping you'd talk to her sometime this week and maybe give counseling a try."

Ember stood stoically, not believing this was her life. She watched Kendall shower without a care in the world and noted water cascading over the black and orange butterfly tattoo on her right shoulder.

Kandice, Kendall's twin, had the same tattoo on her left shoulder and somehow, Ember had forgotten all about her fiancée's twin and the subtle differences in their body art.

The weight of her deception came crashing down like an avalanche. At that moment, she realized that some secrets were too dangerous to keep hidden, and some truths too painful to speak. So, like a child who feared getting reprimanded, Ember lied to save herself. "Sure babe, I'll talk to her."

Stripping herself of the Albany State sweatshirt and jeans, Ember prepared a performance worthy of an Oscar. She tossed the clothes aside and stepped into the shower behind Kendall, falling into a false sense of peace as the steam from the hot shower enveloped them.

Beneath her surface, Ember's nerves crackled with palpable tension as she went through the motions and washed her body. Every word Kendall spoke sounded distorted and the fleeting glances she tossed over her shoulder were a potential threat to the fragile facade she had constructed.

Absent-mindedly, she followed Kendall out of the glass-enclosed space and reached for a towel. They dried off in silence, each lost in their own thoughts. Kendall was worried about Ember's growing PTSD symptoms while Ember was worried about keeping a secret from the one she loved.

After settling in bed, with her front to Kendall's back, Ember's thoughts raced a mile a minute. She tossed and turned to get comfortable, but her mental state wouldn't let her be great.

Looking over her shoulder, Kendall asked, "Are you okay, babe? You seem tense and anxious."

Instead of answering, Ember reached around to Kendall's front, spread her legs, and traced the outline of her yoni. Kendall's head fell back as she writhed against Ember's finger. Before things escalated, Ember rolled Kendall onto her back and slipped between a pair of long slender legs. Skillfully, she massaged the plump pearl currently salivating for her. Simultaneously, she used her tongue to penetrate Kendall, sending her lover on a pleasurable rollercoaster. Kendall reveled in the pleasure, writhing in sweet agony as if Ember's tongue had set her soul on fire.

"Yeeesss baby, right there," Kendall hissed while grinding against her face until she came. Ember drank from her fountain until the well ran dry.

"Wow, babe. Tell me how you really feel," Kendall joked with a chuckle.

With stickiness between her thighs, Kendall slipped out of bed, heading for the bathroom where she used a washcloth to wipe the mess. Once done, she glanced in the corner to find Ember's clothes strewn across the floor. *I don't know how many times I've told that girl to clean up after herself*, she thought while picking up the clothes.

She tossed them in the hamper in the corner and prepared to walk away until a piece of white plastic caught her eye. She ambled over, slipped the card out of Ember's pocket, and inspected it with curiosity. It was an ID badge for the same company her sister worked for.

As a branding consultant, Ember's job required her to work with various companies, so it wasn't uncommon for her to have access badges to different buildings, so she placed the badge on the counter and walked back into the bedroom.

There, she found Ember lying with her back turned. She smiled sweetly, assuming her life was all rainbows and sunshine. Her bubble burst seconds later when she eyed the news playing out on television with closed captions. As she walked further into the room, Kendall's gaze zoned in on the sixty-five-inch television mounted on the wall where she read the words, "Breaking News."

Videos of a crime scene in the Legacy Branding building played in the background as the anchorwoman presented the segment. Fully invested in the story, Kendall grabbed the remote from the nightstand and increased the volume. "In a shocking turn of events, the bodies of esteemed businessman Quentin Daily, his assistant and apparent mistress, Hazel Cromer, and the twin sister of a local police detective, Kendall Jordan, were discovered earlier today in what authorities are describing as a crime of passion. More details to come as this story develops."

"Ahhhh! No, no, no, no, no!"

Kendall's scream caused Ember to jerk from her position and shoot upright in bed. She turned in the direction of her fiancée and scrambled from the bed, wondering what her cause of pain was. When she followed Kendall's eyes, her knees fell weak. Oh shit!

For a moment, time stood still. It wasn't until Kendall fell to her knees and covered her face with her hands that Ember rushed to her aid, flinching from the deafening cries erupting from her throat.

Rubbing her back for comfort, Ember tried in vain to console Kendall, but there were no words to rid her of the pain she felt, and what made matters even worse was knowing she was the one who caused it.

"I need to get out of here and see what's going on," Kendall said through sobs. She shoved Ember aside and rushed to her feet. She retreated to the bathroom to get dressed and head to the station. At the sink counter, she stopped and picked up the Legacy Branding ID badge and ran back into the bedroom to ask, "Did you see anything out of the ordinary when you were there today?"

"When I was where, babe?"

"Legacy Branding. You were there today, right? I found the badge in your pocket," Kendall told her, holding up the plastic card. "Did you see anything or anyone that looked suspicious?"

Nearly every breath in Ember's body flooded from her lungs.

Kaine had managed to save her once by remembering the flash drive but having the ID badge was an issue she'd have to deal with on her own. As she stood avoiding Kendall's eyes, Ember tried hard to think of a lie that would appease both her conscience and her woman. Unfortunately, the lie didn't come to her quickly enough and Kendall became leery.

Stepping into Ember's personal space, Kendall asked, "Is there something you're not telling me, Em? You've been acting strange ever since you got home. What's going on? Do you know something or not?"

The walls seemingly closed in and the tension in the air was suffocating. Ember's erratic breathing showed in the rapid rise and fall of her chest, and it didn't go unnoticed by Kendall. As a detective, she was privy to the meaning of certain body language, especially liars, and in that moment, she knew Ember was withholding viable information.

"Ember Carson, if you know something about this shit, you better start talking. Now!"

"I—I don't know anything, babe, but we'll figure it out together. Let me just run and grab something to put on and I'll go with you," Ember stuttered, walking towards the bathroom closet.

As she fumbled around cursing herself for the mess she made, Kendall walked to the nightstand to grab her phone and service weapon. Her hands trembled something fierce and every fiber of her being told her that something was amiss. She didn't make it to be a detective because of her good looks and charm. She made it because of her hard work, diligence, and relentless pursuit of the truth. And that's exactly what she planned to get.

As soon as Ember walked back into the room dressed in a dark grey sweatshirt and matching joggers, Kendall turned. With her pistol aimed at Ember, she repeated her question reluctantly, fearing the answer. "Do you know what happened to my sister at Legacy Branding?"

Arms raised in surrender, Ember bit her trembling lip to keep the tears at bay. "Kendall, what are you doing? I told you I don't know anything."

"You're lying. You only call me Kendall when you've fucked up."

"Baby, I—"

"Do not 'baby' me right now! Start...fuckin'...talking, or I swear to God, I will kill you and ask questions later," she confessed, tightening her grip on the gun.

Knowing Kendall didn't make idol threats, Ember found herself stuck between life and death. Her heart rate skyrocketed because she knew things would end badly for her whether she told the truth or not. The only thing left to do was take accountability and face the consequences.

Pulling a pistol of her own from her waistband, Ember quickly took aim and fired a single shot into Kendall's chest. The impact sent her lover to the floor with a thud. After tossing the gun on the bed, Ember slowly walked over and stood over Kendall's body to say, "I'm sorry baby, but I can't take the fall for this. It was an accident, and I never meant for it to happen."

Looking down on her beloved, Ember didn't see what she expected to see. Her eyes bulged in surprise, and it was then that she realized she'd made a grave mistake.

Kendall's bulletproof vest saved her, and she was grateful for her intuition telling her not to trust Ember's word.

Staring at each other knowingly, both women scrambled for their weapons and within seconds, a single shot rang out.

THE END

Thank You

Dear Reader,

Thank you for joining us on this journey through *The Freestyle Cypher*. We are deeply grateful for your time and support. Your choice to explore our collective work means the world to us.

We hope you found inspiration, entertainment, and perhaps a new perspective within these pages. Your feedback is incredibly valuable to us, and we would love to hear your thoughts. If you enjoyed the anthology, please consider leaving a review. Your insights help us grow and reach more readers like you.

Thank you for being a part of our literary community.

Sincerely,

The Authors of The Freestyle Cypher

Acknowledgements

The Freestyle Cypher, this volume, the previous and any that follow, would not be possible without Ebony Evans. She is the EyeCU Reading & Social Network Book Club president & founder, EyeCU Reading and Chatting Founder/Administrator, an author and creative visionary. Without the idea of "Freestyle Fridays" there would be no us/this. Thank you, Ebony for giving many authors a platform, exposure, and your unwavering support.

Freestyle Friday has birthed many novels, novellas, and anthologies. I can speak for myself when I say, it has served as a way to stoke the writing fire within, many times. Keep being you and keep driving and inspiring us.

About the Authors

Kaylynn Hunt, known as The Freestyle Queen in the EyeCu Reading and Chatting world, has penned over 100 freestyles since its inseption. She is an author in many genres and has a knack for crafting a twist you don't see coming.

She is a Detroit native that writes the city as the backdrop to many of her stories. Check out Kaylynn's many titles on Amazon or via her website. KaylynnHunt.com Keep up to date with new releases and writing new via Kaylynn's newletter.

Award winning and best selling author **Tanisha Stewart** was born and raised in Springfield, Massachusetts. She graduated with a Bachelor of Science in Psychology and Sociology in  2009, as well as a Master of Psychology in 2011. She is a college professor, teaching psychology (which she loves). In addition to her career as a lecturer, Tanisha has been writing for as long as she can remember, creating realistic story lines, relatable characters, and multi-layered plots that almost everyone can enjoy. She also takes part in hobbies such as performing rap and spoken word for various audiences.

Tanisha not only demonstrates a passion for writing through her vivid story lines; she is also committed to helping other writers succeed. She offers author coaching, editing, formatting, and ghostwriting services to help aspiring authors get their work off the ground, and to see it through to completion. In addition to this, she hosts Book Optimization and Amazon Ads courses. You can find out more about Tanisha and these services at www.tanishastewartauthor.com.

Meet **Toni Larue'**, the creative force behind captivating suspense novels that have kept countless readers on the edge of their seats. The Bay Area native introduces a refreshing and rejuvenating element to the thriller genre by deftly crafting compelling narratives and evocative African American characters  that linger long after you put the book down.

Tap into all of her titles on Amazon.

E. Raye Turonek is a married mother of five. The Detroit, Michigan native resides with her husband and family in a small  rural town in Michigan. Since releasing her debut literary work, Compelled to Murder, in 2016 the author has penned five additional novels and also publishes a monthly newsletter highlighting all things literary— as well as astrology forecasts. This multifaceted author is looking to fulfill the reader's need for a sensational experience that won't be forgotten.

Check out all of her titles on Amazon also check out her website for up to date information. www.erayebook.com

Octavia Grant discovered her love of creative writing at the  age of sixteen. She began writing professionally in 2016, two years later she decided to take the reins of her literary career and became an Independent Author. As an Independent Author, Octavia has penned over 30 novels. She's been interviewed by Narrator iiKane, interviewed by Literary Reviewer and Movie Commentator Tamara Walker of Tam Telling Tales, featured in magazines WYB Lifestyle, Voyage Jacksonville, Canvas Rebel, named in 160 Black Women In Horror as well as the winner of the It's Lit Award for Best Black Mystery/Suspense.

You can check out all of Octavia's titles on Amazon or her website.

Keira N. James is a thriller author hailing from Danville, GA.

While the U.S. Navy once claimed her dedication, her heart has always belonged to the world of words.

As a devoted mother raising her son, she knows that the best adventure is the one called parenthood. When she's not chasing plot twists in her novels, Keira is raising her teenager, teaching him the ropes of becoming a productive member of society.

Keira's love affair with books started long before her writing journey began. She'd lose herself in the pages of gripping tales, and now, she's the one crafting those twists, giving readers the same excitement she once enjoyed as a bookworm.

With her dedication and determination, she's set her sights on impacting readers, providing exceptional literary experiences, and the coveted NYT Bestseller's list, and it's only a matter of time before she conquers it.

So, if you're looking for heart-pounding, page-turning suspense, Keira N. James is your go-to author. Dive into her world of thrillers and get ready for a literary escape like no other.

All Keira's titles can be found on Amazon as well as her website, www.thekeiranjames.com.